"YOU WERE NOT SAVING
THE HONOR OF A VIRGIN...

when you saved me from those two cockroaches, señor." Juanita hesitated a moment, then said softly, "Do you not wish to know why I speak of this now?"

Longarm smiled. "I think I understand. It was that long ride...with your arms about my waist. The closeness..."

Her eyes brightened in gratitude. "Yes," she cried, "it was that! Oh, Longarm, I think I die if you do not take me!"

She was out of her soogan and beside him in an instant, fitting her long, unashamedly naked body close against his....

Also in the **LONGARM** series
from Jove

— TABOR EVANS —

LONGARM

IN THE BIG BEND

A JOVE BOOK

LONGARM IN THE BIG BEND

A Jove Book / published by arrangement with
the author

PRINTING HISTORY
Jove edition / December 1982

ISBN: 0-515-06251-0

Jove books are published by Jove Publications, Inc.,
200 Madison Avenue, New York, N. Y. 10016. The words
"A JOVE BOOK" and the "J" with sunburst are trademarks
belonging to Jove Publications, Inc.

PRINTED IN THE UNITED STATES OF AMERICA

Prologue

Captain Miles Winthrop was worried. Hell, he was scared silly. Apaches he could handle and he never minded punishing the damned *rurales,* but what was overtaking him at that moment put the fear of the Lord God Jehovah in him.

An awesome wall of thundering, climbing water was overtaking his flimsy raft. This notion of his to raft down the Rio Grande through the Big Bend country had tempted him for years. He had heard it could be done, and he had bet a few of his cronies back at Presidio that he could do it. But at this moment, as he poled frantically toward shore, he realized what a pure damn fool he had been.

Earlier, he had heard the mutter of thunder and had

seen the flickering tongues of flame as the rain-swollen clouds above the Chisos Mountains discharged their tons of water. Now the swollen river was rolling down upon him, eager to swallow him up, then spit him out for his impertinence.

The captain was not a small man, and his powerful figure strained mightily as he poled his raft toward the mouth of a canyon he saw yawning before him. As his raft swept closer, a tall sentinel of rock loomed out of the water beside the canyon's entrance.

Abruptly, the raft heaved under his feet, throwing him forward onto its ribbed surface. He glanced back and saw at once how hopeless his cause was. The surging wall of water was nearly on him. The raft continued to lift under him. Flinging his pole away, he searched frantically for something to grab. But there was nothing and, like a live thing, the raft lifted out of the water, then flipped, hurtling the captain backward through the air. He felt himself knifing head-first into the water and felt the warm, heavy water sucking him down. Pulling himself back up through the tumultuous water, he surfaced, then struck out for the canyon entrance. But the fierce current caught him up.

The towering finger of rock he had noticed earlier tipped crazily as the current spilled him sideways. Turgid with silt and debris, the water spun him like a cork. Again he was sucked below the surface, one more piece of flotsam in the midst of branches and small chunks of soil and debris. With numbing force, he struck a submerged wall of rock. At the same time, he felt the current release him. Turning his eyes upward, he caught sight of the dim light far above him and began to pull himself up toward it.

When he broke the surface, the first thing he saw was that rocky sentinel looming out of the water. But it was well behind him now as the river swept him along. Paddling frantically, he turned his head just in time to see the unyielding surface of a canyon wall rushing toward him. He managed to turn himself completely and fling out his hands a moment before he struck the wall, cushioning the impact somewhat.

Then, as the river started to batter him unmercifully, he managed to reach up and grab hold of a craggy outcropping of rock just above him. There was a ledge above the outcropping. Reaching up desperately, he strained mightily to pull himself up onto it. But by this time he was too far gone. His hands were raw and his arms were as heavy as anvils. The water continued to pound him, grinding him brutally into the rock face, and he felt himself slipping back into the roaring maelstrom.

A powerful hand reached down, grabbed his right wrist, and hauled him up onto the ledge. The captain rolled over, gasping, and looked up to see a sturdily built old man leaning close to him, wide-eyed concern—or was it fear?—on his black face.

"Thank God!" the captain managed. "You saved my guts! But where in hell did you come from?"

"Come with me, mastah!" the darky pleaded. "They're after me!"

Struggling to his feet, the captain asked, "Who? Who's after you?"

"The colonel, suh! The colonel!"

Without further explanation, the black man led the captain along the ledge, then up a precipitous slope until they were far above the still churning river. Hurrying around a huge boulder, the Negro ducked ahead of the

3

captain into a high, narrow cave.

Collapsing on the cavern's floor in total exhaustion, the captain sucked air deep into his laboring lungs. Muddy water still clung to his clothing. He felt heavy and sodden. When he ran his hand through his hair, he could feel the grit. But he was alive, and that was the true miracle.

He glanced up at the Negro, who was crouching now at the cave entrance, peering fearfully back down the trail. Wearily, the captain got to his feet and approached the man who had saved his life. At his approach, the black man turned, a momentary apprehension in his eyes. The captain smiled and held out his hand.

"My name's Miles Winthrop," he said. "What's yours?"

"Ben," the man replied.

"Just Ben?"

"Yassuh. Just Ben. Some calls me Old Ben. But my mastah, the colonel, he just calls me Ben."

"What's that you say? Your master?"

The darky bowed his head quickly. "Yassuh, that's right. My mastah, the colonel. I tole you! He's a-comin' aftah me. I struck one of his captains, I did. He don't like that. But I'm sick of beatin's, so I run off to this here cave."

The captain stood back a minute to look at the man who had saved his life. Ben was a skinny Negro in his late fifties, his close-cropped curly hair already turning gray. His features were sharp and intelligent. On his way up to this cave, Ben had moved along swiftly enough, but with a decided limp. And now some crazy colonel was after him? And this darky was calling him his master?

The captain shook his head in disbelief. "Ben," the

captain said, "where you been all this time? You ain't got no master now. The slaves have all been set free."

Ben's eyes widened, then as swiftly narrowed in suspicion. "Now how could that be, suh? The colonel, he ain't done tole us nothin' of the sort. Ever since we been here, he's been a-promisin' us our freedom soon's the War's over."

For a moment the captain had difficulty following the darky's words. It was too incredible. But the look on Ben's face convinced him that this poor old Negro was absolutely sincere.

"Ben!" the captain said earnestly, leaning close to emphasize his words. "The War is over! My God, man, it's been over these past fifteen years! And even before it was, Lincoln freed the slaves! Whoever this colonel of yours is, he ain't got no right to hold you or any other Negroes in bondage."

Ben took an uncertain step backward. It was obvious he wanted to believe the captain, but what the captain was saying was so incredible that Ben was afraid the man he had pulled from the river was out of his head.

"You sure do tell a lie convincin', suh," Ben said, nodding anxiously, obviously hoping to placate the captain. "Yassuh, you sure does!" Then he smiled, and the captain saw that most of Ben's teeth were gone, knocked out, more than likely, since those that remained were brilliant white and looked strong.

"Ben," the captain said, stepping back, his face suddenly cold, "are you callin' me a liar?"

"Oh, no, suh!" cried Ben in sudden, almost abject capitulation. "I sure didn't mean to do that!"

A fear so abject it was sickening to contemplate filled the darky's countenance. The old Negro took a hesitant step backward, and in that single action, the captain realized that to this Negro the War Between the States was still in progress and Lincoln's Emancipation Proclamation had simply never taken place.

"Ben," the captain said gently, taking the darky by the arm and leading him over to a sheltered section of the cave, "why don't you tell me about this here colonel of yours?"

Ben looked for a long moment at the captain, then shrugged and, squatting down facing him, began talking. At first, the captain found the Negro's story as difficult to believe as Ben had found the captain's assertion that the War was over. But the captain's incredulity soon gave way to belief, then wonder, and finally to a deep, abiding anger.

When the old Negro had finished his story and the captain had in turn finally managed to convince the astonished man of the truth of what he had told him earlier, the river below them had grown much quieter.

But now that it was quiet, they were able to hear the distant shouts of searchers and the eager yap of hounds on the scent. Ben cowered back into the shadows of the cave, his eyes wide with fear. Ben's master wanted his slave back, it seemed.

Captain Miles Winthrop felt only a growing sense of rage and frustration as he cowered, like Ben, in the silence of the cave. The sound of the search party grew steadily louder, until there was no longer any doubt in his mind that the hounds had found Ben's trail.

With a deep sigh, Ben got to his feet. "I guess I better go back down and meet the colonel, suh. They come up here, they'll find you. They don't like people from the outside. I seen what they do to them that comes in here

6

uninvited. You best stay back out of sight."

"They'll beat you, Ben."

"Yassuh, they will. But I been beat before."

"Come with me. We'll get out of here together."

"How we gonna do that, suh?"

"The river, Ben. Can you swim?"

The Negro nodded.

"Good."

Miles took off his boots, walked to the cave entrance, and looked down at the still swift waters far below. It was a long drop; but he had no assurance that staying up here and waiting for this mad colonel was going to do anything for his health, either. At least this way there was a chance that Ben would finally escape his incredible servitude.

Ben moved up beside him and peered down at the water. "That sure is a long way down, suh. You sure you strong enough? You was pretty tired when I pulled you out."

"I'm not tired any more, Ben. But I sure as hell am angry."

Ben took a deep breath, then flashed his few remaining teeth at the captain. "I'm ready, suh!"

Before the captain could reply, however, a shot rang out from the trail below them. The old Negro buckled, then sank to the ground. Glancing down the trail, the captain saw two men in Confederate uniforms standing on the ledge below them, rifles to their shoulders. Another rifle cracked, and the captain felt a slug snick past his cheek. He waited no longer and dove off the cliff.

Knifing cleanly into the warm water, he surfaced quickly and struck out for the opposite shore, allowing the swift current to carry him along. The soldiers sent

7

a few more shots after him, but he was soon well out of range. Grimly determined to survive somehow so that he could return and make the colonel pay, the captain pulled steadily toward the far side of the river.

He was just about certain he was going to make it when he was swept around the bend and saw the seething rapids just ahead of him. He redoubled his efforts to reach the far shore, but in a numbingly short time he was swept into the violent, choppy waters. Abruptly, he was flung against a rock. He lost consciousness momentarily and was only dimly aware of being dragged under by the fierce current.

Shaking his head to clear it, he surfaced and began paddling frantically, keeping his head up and his arms flailing as he was flung headlong into the roaring chute.

Chapter 1

Billy Vail mopped his florid face with his handkerchief
and peered with some impatience across the desk at Longarm. "I know just how it sounds, damn it!"

Longarm smiled and held his hand up to placate the
exasperated marshal. "I didn't say I didn't believe you,
Chief. Go on. I'm listening."

Vail mopped his brow and smiled weakly. A man who
was once as tough as old saddle leather, the marshal had
long since gone to suet—a constant reminder to Longarm
to keep on the move and stay away from desks.

Longarm unwrapped a cheroot and lit it, then leaned
back in the chief's red morocco leather armchair. The
banjo clock on the wall indicated nine o'clock. Longarm
had arrived only a few moments before. The fact that

Vail had not brought Longarm's tardiness to his attention had alerted the tall lawman. Something was up—something very unusual. And that was fine with Longarm. He was anxious to put the coal dust and horse manure of this mile-high city well behind him. He had played enough poker and chased enough perfumed skirts. Now he craved some real action.

"I guess it's me that finds it hard to believe, at that," Vail confessed unhappily. "Let me start at the beginning." He pawed through the drifts of correspondence that cluttered his desk and pulled forth a heavy manila folder and opened it. Glancing quickly through its contents to refresh his memory, he peered across his desk at Longarm.

"That account I gave you is all in here. Maybe you should read it yourself. But this crazy story is not the only thing that has brought Washington into this. For some time now the Customs Bureau in Washington has been getting nervous about the amount of opium showing up in Matamoros and slipping across the border into Texas. You know how it is—Washington wants its share of the pie and this stuff is getting in duty free, too much of it lately to ignore."

"So what else is new?"

"I know. I know. But this new traffic is in addition to some other traffic that has always bothered the Rangers—cotton, good quality cotton, and beef cattle—all of it showing up in Matamoros, then disappearing not long after to turn up in markets across the border. The thing is, the Mexicans themselves don't have the resources or the inclination, it seems, to produce all this cotton or this quality beef, and now this opium is like the straw that broke the camel's back. Where in hell is this stuff coming from? That's what Washington wants to know."

"So send in the Army. They'll find out soon enough. One of Diaz's honchos has gotten himself a spread and is putting the locals to work on it, more than likely."

Billy Vail sighed. "It's not as simple as that. The Diaz dictatorship is pretty touchy about the United States sending Army troops into their country. We don't want another war with Mexico. Not just yet, we don't." He paused, then leaned back in his seat, eyeing Longarm shrewdly. "And now comes this report from Presidio concerning Captain Winthrop. So you see where it puts us."

Longarm sighed. "I see where it puts me—or where you're trying to put me. You want me to go down there and get in touch with this captain, do you?"

"That won't be possible. He was chewed up pretty bad by the rocks as he was swept through the Big Bend. He died soon after he was brought back to Presidio. This account of his was recorded by his commanding officer while the captain was on his deathbed."

Longarm's eyebrows went up. That put a different complexion on things. A dying man does not usually spend his last moments concocting a cock-and-bull story. "I see," he replied thoughtfully. "But you do want me to go down there and check this out."

"I don't want you to. Washington does. I know what happens whenever you get near the *rurales*—you start another war with Mexico. But they want my best man in Denver to check this out and, damn it, Longarm, that's you."

"I'm flattered. I shouldn't be, but I am."

"Never mind that. How soon can you leave?"

11

"Right now."

Vail smiled somewhat crookedly. He leaned forward in his chair, resting his elbows on his cluttered desk. "I can understand your haste, I think."

"Now what do you mean by that, Chief?"

"I heard you had a little trouble last night at the Windsor."

Longarm took the cheroot out of his mouth. "You heard right. A fellow from back East took exception to my skill at cards." Longarm smiled slightly. "And the way his lady friend admired that skill."

Billy Vail shook his head slowly, evincing both exasperation and envy. "So that meant you had to walk off with the lady too, did it?"

"Chief, I never insult a lady. And have you ever considered what an insult it is to a pretty woman to be turned down by a handsome, well-turned-out gentleman such as myself? Besides, her escort had by this time become somewhat of an embarrassment. He handled his liquor as badly as he handled his cards."

Patiently, Vail ran his hands through his gray, thinning hair. "Do you happen to know who this dandy is, Longarm?"

"Cecil something-or-other."

Vail sighed. "That something-or-other is Benton. He's Cecil Benton, Senator Boris Benton's son, and the girl you left with is his fiancée."

"Was," Longarm corrected. "She promised me she would have nothing further to do with that milksop. And I do believe she will keep that promise."

Vail got to his feet. "Well then, I guess that's as good a reason as any for getting you out of Denver on the first train south. As soon as I get your travel vouchers ready, get your possibles and move out. There's a train leaving at one this afternoon."

"Let me look through that folder while I'm waiting for that clerk of yours," Longarm suggested. "I'd like to read what this captain had to say. His story sounds crazy enough, I admit, but I suppose what he says could be true."

Vail handed Longarm the folder, then hurried around his desk and left the office. Puffing contentedly on his cheroot, Longarm leaned back in the leather armchair and commenced to read.

He was reading Captain Miles Winthrop's account over a third time, the cheroot dead in his mouth, when Marshal Vail returned with his travel vouchers.

Less than an hour later, having packed his possibles in his carpetbag, Longarm turned his attention to his firepower. Withdrawing his double-action Colt Model T .44-40 from his cross-draw rig, he swung out the gate and shook the five rounds into his palm, then dropped them into the side pocket of his brown tweed frock coat and examined the Colt's firing pin critically. Black powder left a gummy deposit after only a few rounds, Longarm knew, and a fouled firing pin was not much help in a pinch. Satisfied that his weapon was clean, he dropped it back into his rig, then turned his attention to a second weapon he kept cunningly concealed on his person, his double-barreled derringer.

Connected to his watch by a gold chain, the weapon served as a fob, one that had proven itself as a most deadly surprise to more than one unsuspecting gunslick. He lifted out the derringer, unclipped the chain from its brass butt, and examined the derringer closely. Then he

13

dropped it back into his left vest pocket and reached for his snuff-brown Stetson.

Placing it carefully on his head, he leaned close to the mirror and tweaked the ends of his longhorn mustache, then lifted his carpetbag from his bed and started for the door. The sound of running footsteps in the hallway outside caused him to pull up. They were too heavy to be his landlady's, he realized, and he was not surprised when they halted outside his door. A sharp, anxious knock followed.

"Who is it?" Longarm asked.

"It's me! Jeanette!"

With a soft curse, Longarm flung his carpetbag back onto his bed and pulled open the door. Jeanette, tears streaming down her face, flung herself into his room and buried her face in his shoulder. The tall lawman held her sobbing form closely for a moment, then reached past her and swung the door shut, after which he led her gently over to his bed and sat her down.

Jeanette kept her head down as she dabbed at her eyes with a lace handkerchief. "Oh, Longarm!" she wailed. "I'm so ashamed! I didn't mean to come to you like this, but I had no choice. He *struck* me—the cad!"

"Who?" Longarm asked, though he didn't really have any doubt that Jeanette was talking about Cecil Benton.

"Cecil! He came to my room less than an hour ago and demanded to know where I had gone with you. When I told him I was not going to marry him and that it was no business of his where I had gone, he began to beat me. I managed to break free of him and run out of the hotel." She looked up at Longarm, her eyes wide in sudden alarm. "Oh, forgive me, Longarm! I know I

14

shouldn't have come here, but I didn't know where else to go."

"You think he might have followed you?"

"Oh, yes! I'm certain of it. What shall we do, Longarm?"

"I don't think you should do anything except pull yourself together, Jeanette. As for me, I have a few minutes to spare. Why don't I just settle down and wait for this ex-fiancé of yours. There's just one question."

Wiping her eyes, she peered fearfully at Longarm. "Yes, Longarm?"

"Is he armed?"

"Yes, I think so. He has one of his father's dueling pistols."

"I see."

"Please forgive me, Longarm. I guess it *was* wicked of me, wasn't it, to go off with you last night? I just don't know what got into me!"

Despite her tear-streaked countenance, Jeanette was still an incredibly lovely young woman. Her brows thick, her eyes bright blue, her pile of rich auburn hair wound about her head like a magnificent crown, her rosy lips full and passionate, she was a prize any man would give his life and fortune to claim as his own, and Longarm found it easy to understand why the loss of such unblemished loveliness would send Cecil Denton into a rage.

Longarm leaned close and kissed Jeanette lightly on her cheek. "Yes, you do know what got into you. And, what's more, for me it was worth it—whatever the cost."

"Oh, Longarm, you're so gallant. And it was worth it to me, as well."

The sound of heavy, deliberate footsteps approaching his door alerted them both. Glancing at Jeanette, Longarm pressed his forefinger to his lips, then got cautiously to his feet and walked silently across the room to the door. As the footsteps paused outside the door, Longarm took his Colt, then closed his left hand over the doorknob and waited.

There was a sudden, angry pounding on the door.

"Jeanette!" came Cecil Benton's furious voice. "I know you're in there! The landlady told me which room is Long's. Come out of there now or I'll kick this door in!"

Twisting the knob, Longarm yanked the door open. As it slammed against the wall, Longarm struck down at Benton's right hand with his Colt and knocked from it the huge pistol Benton was holding. As Benton yelped in pain, Longarm grabbed him by the front of his shirt and pulled him into the room.

With an angry, petulant snarl, the fellow spun around and flung himself at Longarm. Longarm stepped back and cuffed him in the face. The force of the slap caused Benton to rock back, his eyes watering. It did not stop him, however. Like an infuriated child, he lowered his head and ran blindly at Longarm. Slipping deftly to one side, Longarm put his right foot out. Benton tripped over it and went slamming head-first into the wall. Stunned, he slipped to the floor, then rolled over to gaze up through bleary eyes at Longarm.

Longarm leaned close to young Benton. "Now you listen to me, boy. If I ever hear of you laying a hand on Jeanette again, I'll come after you—no matter where you are and no matter who you think you are. Is that clear?"

The young man's eyes narrowed craftily. He moistened his lips and barely nodded. "I heard you," he said, his voice a cold rasp. "I won't touch her. She's just a damned slut, anyway!"

Longarm leaned close and slapped Benton hard.

Tears of rage squeezed out of Benton's eyes. "I won't touch her," he repeated, his voice nasty. "That's a promise. But I'll get you, Long. And *that's* a promise. No matter where you go and no matter how tough you think you are. Every time you go past a dark alley, I want you to think of me. Because one of those times I'll be there waiting—with a sawed-off shotgun. Is *that* clear?"

Longarm straightened up and stepped back from Benton. There was an unmistakable gleam of madness in the young man's eyes. A cold chill ran down Longarm's spine. This milksop had become suddenly a very deadly jasper indeed. Unaccustomed to being stood up to, the experience had torn away what little civilized veneer still clung to him.

Benton was of a type Longarm had seen often enough. The West was filling up with such dangerous misfits— most of them from well-to-do families. Their indulgent parents had created monsters and, no longer able to cope with them, had sent them packing to the West. Cecil Benton was one of them.

"Get out of here, Benton," Longarm said, stepping away from the young man. "Get out of here before I change my mind. And remember what I said. Leave Jeanette alone or you'll hear from me."

Slowly young Benton got to his feet. He was not over twenty-two or twenty-three, Longarm surmised. He might even have been handsome if his sharp, clean features hadn't had such a constantly sullen expression, and if the thin, cruel line of his mouth had not hardened into a perpetual sneer. His mean eyes were slate-gray, his hair a ratty brown.

Benton slouched for the door. "And you remember what I said, too, Long. I have friends. And money. All I need. I'll wait until I'm sure. Just think of me every time you go past a dark alley."

"Get out of here, Cecil!" Jeanette cried. "Get out! You're a horrid little worm!"

Benton flung the door open and stalked out. Longarm followed after him and closed the door firmly. As Benton's footsteps receded down the hallway, he turned to Jeanette.

"He's a worm, all right. What I'd like to know is, how in tarnation did you ever manage to get engaged to the likes of him?"

"My family thought it would be a fine match for me." She sighed wearily.

"I have to move out, Jeanette," Longarm told her. "I've a train to catch at one. But I don't like the idea of leaving you alone in this town with that one on the loose. Do you think you'll be all right?"

"Yes, if you'll take me back to my hotel room. I'll lock Cecil out and wait for my brother to come for me. As soon as I get back to the hotel, I'll wire him. He's in St. Louis. I'll be all right now, I'm sure."

"Good," said Longarm, snatching up his carpetbag and snugging his hat back down onto his head.

As the train pulled into Presidio, Longarm recognized at once the sun-bleached, somnolent look of the Texas border town. It was a familiar, if depressing, sight. The flagpoles in front of the Army post's headquarters were

visible on a small rise behind the town, and as Longarm
stood on the platform between the coaches and waited
for the train to come to a halt, he glimpsed more than
a few uniformed men moving along the town's narrow,
dusty streets. They were keeping within the shadows, he
noticed grimly, well out of the sun's stark, blasting im-
print.

The coaches ground to a halt. The conductor hopped
down, placing his stool on the platform before the lawman. Longarm swung down and started across the depot
platform, heading for an officer he saw waiting in the
shadows of the depot roof.

Pulling up in front of him, Longarm took out a cheroot
and offered it to the man. "Lieutenant Sanders?"

The man took the cheroot and then nodded. "And I
reckon you'd be Deputy Marshal Long—come all the
way from Denver."

"That's right."

"Come with me, Marshal," Sanders said, lighting the
cheroot. "The captain's waiting."

"Maybe we could stop somewhere to wet our whistle
before that. I'm as dry as a rattlesnake's belly."

"Don't worry," the lieutenant replied with a quick
grin. "The captain's got his own stock. And it's a damn
sight safer than the rotgut they sell in town."

Turning to move off with the lieutenant, Longarm
thought he caught sight of a furtive figure dashing from
the train into the shadows beyond the water tower further
up the track. Longarm pulled up quickly to get a better
look. He couldn't be sure, of course—not at this distance—but the way that fellow moved sure as hell reminded him of the way Cecil Benton scuttled about.

Shading his eyes, Longarm squinted through the blazing sunlight at the area about the water tower, but caught no further movement at all.

"What is it?" the lieutenant inquired.

"Nothing, I guess," said Longarm, starting up once again. "In this heat that landscape plays a few tricks on a man's eyes."

"You've been in these parts before, then."

"Yes, I have," Longarm replied wearily as they moved out of the protection of the depot and the heavy weight of the sun fell upon his back. He sure as hell had.

But, as he walked, Longarm felt more than the sun's pressure on his back. He felt two eyes, malignant and hateful. Young Benton's eyes. The sun had not been playing tricks on him, he knew full well.

That crazy young kid had followed him all the way to this border town.

Captain Martin Wellman was a tall, blocky man in his early fifties with a thick mane of snow-white hair, a well-trimmed and heavily-seamed face dominated by a nose as powerful and memorable as that of any Apache chieftain. If it were not for the fierce light in his blue eyes and the bold white mustache that coiled, walrus-like, down over his mouth, Captain Wellman could easily have passed for an Indian.

He rose to greet Longarm and gave him a hearty handshake. Then, true to the lieutenant's promise, as soon as the three of them were seated comfortably around his desk, the captain produced a fresh bottle of whiskey from a lower drawer. Filling each of their glasses generously, Wellman saluted Longarm and his mission, then settled back to answer any questions the lawman might have.

"I guess my first question," Longarm said, after passing around his cheroots and lighting one up himself, "is, what in blazes was Miles Winthrop doing in the Big Bend, anyway?"

The lieutenant cleared his throat nervously. "I'm afraid that was my fault, Marshal."

"Your fault?"

"In a manner of speaking, yes. We had a bet on. I bet him a month's pay he couldn't pole his way through the Big Bend country. You might even say I dared him to do it."

"Don't be too hard on yourself, Lieutenant," said the captain. "You know damn well that Miles was determined to make that journey sooner or later."

"And what was it that prompted him to make it now?" Longarm persisted.

"I guess I can answer that," said the captain. He smiled and puffed contentedly on the cheroot Longarm had given him. "We drove Victorio and his damned Apaches from the Big Bend. Not long after, we learned that the son of a bitch had been killed in a skirmish with Mexican troopers at Tres Castillos in northern Chihuahua. I'm not saying we've wiped every Apache out of the Big Bend, but very few of Victorio's band remains."

The lieutenant spoke up then. "As soon as Miles learned this, he started talking up the water route through the Big Bend. He was convinced that a sturdy enough raft and one man who knew how to pole it could make it through. If he was successful, I have no doubt he would have asked for an early discharge and set up a company to use the Rio Grande as part of a land and water route from California to Laredo."

"A foolish notion, we all realize now," the captain

21

continued. "It is expected that soon two railroads will be spanning the Big Bend country. The Texas and Pacific Railroad has already sent surveyors into the Big Bend, I understand."

"And the Southern Pacific will be coming in from the West later," the lieutenant added.

"So Captain Miles Winthrop was on a fool's errand," Longarm commented.

"He loved rivers, Marshal," said the captain thoughtfully. "I guess maybe he was just looking for an excuse to run a raft through that country."

"This story of his. Do you believe it?" asked Longarm.

"About this Colonel Sutpen and that canyon of his?"

"That's right."

"Miles was already in a bad way when I got to his bedside, Marshal, but his head was clear enough," said Captain Wellman. "When I got back to my quarters, I wrote down what he told me as near as I could, word for word. I believe it because Miles told it to me on his deathbed. But I have some trouble with it, I can tell you. And remember, Miles was only telling me what this darky had told him."

"Still," said the lieutenant, "if only half of it were true, it would help to explain a lot. The increase in the opium arriving in Matamoros and finding its way back across the border; the cotton, the beef. It must be grown somewhere in the region, but it is not being grown in Mexico. We've ridden all through that desolate country from Chihuahua to Saltillo and back up to San Vincente. And we've scoured both sides of the Rio Conchos."

The captain grinned at him. "With the *rurales* hot on his trail each time."

Longarm nodded grimly. "My best course, then, is to ride along the river as far as I can, and try to approach

22

this fabled canyon from our side."

"If you can," said the lieutenant. "Following the river through the Big Bend on horseback is not going to be easy. That's the roughest patch of landscape I've ever encountered. At times the river's canyons cut through sheer walls of rock at least sixteen hundred feet high."

The captain nodded his agreement. "I'd say your best bet is Boquillas canyon, Longarm. But you're not going to get to it by land. It's the longest of the Rio's canyons—and the deepest and most inaccessible. The trouble is, there are so many side canyons branching off it that no one has yet been able to reach the main canyon, since that would mean traveling so many hundreds of miles laterally in order to reach it."

"You're right," said Longarm, grinning wryly. "It sounds like rough country."

"If you do make contact with these renegade southerners, Longarm," said the lieutenant, "I suggest you not advertise the fact that you are a deputy U. S. marshal."

"You'll need a story to explain your presence in the area," said the captain, "if this colonel is as tough on strangers as Miles indicated he was."

"First things first," said Longarm, getting to his feet. "I'll need a mount and provisions."

"Of course, Marshal," said the captain, getting to his feet also. "Lieutenant Sanders will see to it that you are provided with everything you need."

"When would you like to start?" asked the lieutenant, getting to his feet also.

"First thing tomorrow morning," said Longarm.

Longarm sat at a small table in a corner of the cantina, observing casually the saloon's crowded interior as he sipped the fiery tequila he had been nursing for the past two hours. The long, narrow room was filled with hard, brutal spikes of laughter, and the shouts and accents of the border, Mexican mixed with English and all shades in between, while the stench of sweaty, unwashed bodies and horse manure hung heavy in the smoky air.

Perspiration stood out on Longarm's forehead and soaked his cotton shirt and frock coat. He could feel the beads of moisture inching down his chest and trickling down his back between his shoulder blades. Its chill load was especially heavy about his waist under the cross-draw rig, but he made no move to loosen it. The Colt's heft was a comfort to him as he sat at the table and watched the batwings swing open and shut.

At the moment he was waiting for this cantina and the streets to clear so that he could start back to his hotel. Somewhere, he was almost certain, between the hotel and this saloon Cecil Benton was waiting for him, crouching in some dark alley as he had promised. Longarm would not avoid meeting him, but he would attempt to talk some sense into him if he could.

But if he couldn't, well . . .

Longarm's attention was diverted suddenly to a scuffle in the far corner of the cantina. He heard the slap of a palm against flesh and saw a grizzled patron rock back, his hand up to his cheek, his eyes blazing in rage.

He had been slapped by one of the cantina's girls. She stood her ground now defiantly, her eyes blazing at her tormentor. She was a Mexican girl with a lovely olive complexion, dark sorrowful eyes, and long black hair worn well down past her shoulders. The cantina's owner was too cheap to provide her or any of the other girls with the usual red spangled dresses, but this one was dressed provocatively enough in a dark skirt short enough to show off her fine ankles and a white blouse which she wore off her shoulders.

The outraged patron was joined by a companion. Together, the two men advanced threateningly on the girl. She stood her ground, her eyes flashing defiance, her hands held out, claw-like, before her.

Shouts of derision were directed at the two men, and a few claimed they were betting on the girl.

Both men were bearded. The one who had just suffered the slap was minus the use of his left eye, which appeared to have been gouged cruelly and deliberately, since there was considerable scar tissue built up around the socket. Both men were dressed poorly, and the second, smaller one had holes worn through the knees of his Levi's. Longarm thought he could smell both men from where he sat.

The fellow with the bad eye reached out and grabbed the girl's wrist. She tried to pull free, but with a cruel, vicious yank, he drew her closer.

As he did so, his companion turned back to appeal to the cantina's owner, who had hurried out from behind the bar at the first sign of trouble. "Come on, Pedro!" the patron wheedled. "Let us have Juanita! What makes her so high and mighty? What've you got her here for?"

Pedro was distraught. "Juanita, she no want to go with you, señors!" he cried. "There are plenty other girls. Wait for Dolores! She is back soon, I promise!"

"We want this one!" said the one-eyed fellow, pulling the struggling girl still closer and forcing a kiss on her cheek.

Juanita struggled bitterly and silently. The one-eyed man reached around and pinched her on the behind. The girl yelped in pain and tried to scratch the man. But he just laughed, grabbed her firmly by the wrists, and drew her to him. Bending her cruelly back, he kissed her again, this time on the lips.

Longarm saw tears standing out on the girl's cheeks. "Hold it!" he said, getting to his feet. His voice had carried impressively.

All eyes in the place turned to regard him. With a weary shrug, Longarm tossed the last of his tequila down his gullet and strode toward the struggling couple.

"Let her go," he said quietly. "She doesn't want to go with you."

"What the hell business is it of yours?" snarled the one-eyed man.

But as he turned his attention to Longarm, he released the girl. She shrank quickly back to the wall, her hand up to her face to ward off any further trouble.

"Aw, let's forget about it, Pete," said the fellow's companion. "We don't want that damn slut nohow."

"Speak for yourself, Jake," Pete snapped, his gaze riveted to Longarm's. "This gent ain't tellin' me who I can take."

"Yes, I am," said Longarm quietly. "You make too much noise. Besides that, maybe if you two would wash up some, you wouldn't have all this trouble. Ever think of that?"

There were more than a few grunts of approval at that assertion. Pete's face went scarlet. With a lightning move, his right hand clawed his sixgun from its holster.

With frantic cries of warning, the patrons ducked for cover. The sound of chairs scraping and tables overturning filled the place. Longarm ducked swiftly to one side and reached across his belly for his own Colt. Pete fired at him, but the shot went high. Longarm crabbed sideways and fired up at the man, but Pete was already in flight along with his buddy.

Laughter filled the place. Shouts of derision were hurled after the two men as they fled. Longarm got to his feet and holstered his weapon. As he started back to his table, Juanita hurried over to him, her large brown eyes filled with gratitude.

"Oh, thank you, señor!"

"That's all right, Juanita," he told her, patting her brown arm. "I could smell those two gents all the way over to my table."

"I am not that kind of woman, señor. I work here for my uncle. I laugh with the men and serve drinks. I do nothing more."

"I ain't a man to go pointing any fingers, ma'am," he said, touching the tip of his hat brim to her in salute. "I don't care what you do here. I just don't like to see any woman treated like that."

"You are very kind, señor."

"Would you like to join me at my table?"

She wanted to say yes, he could tell. But instead she shook her head. "I must go to my room and change this dress. That animal tear it. Thank you, señor."

Longarm slumped into his chair as he watched her disappear into the alley in back of the cantina. It seemed so important to her that he not consider her the same as the other girls who worked in the cantina. *Then what in blazes is she doing here?* he wondered as he slumped back in his chair.

The owner of the cantina hurried over to his table with a bottle of tequila, his dark face alight with gratitude.

"She is a good girl, señor," the owner explained. "I

27

no want she should go with such men. Always when you drink here, it is on the house."

Longarm nodded his thanks. As the owner hurried back to the bar, Longarm cocked his head and stared for a moment at the bottle of tequila. He wondered if he should tempt fate with more of that fiery tonsil varnish.

Then, with a fatalistic shrug, he pulled the bottle toward him and poured himself a fresh drink.

The hour was late. Longarm could not be sure, but it appeared to him that his solitary, somewhat baleful presence had cast a pall over the saloon's patrons, even though they had quite obviously approved of his earlier intervention in behalf of the girl.

Juanita had not returned to the cantina, and the remaining girls had become considerably more subdued. The laughter had gradually died, and now an uneasy quiet hung over the place. The patrons began to drift out. After a while, the clatter of horses' hoofs faded and the street outside became quiet. The barkeep wiped the bar off a second time, glancing over at Longarm as he did so. Longarm nodded silently to the man. The time had come, he realized, for him to leave.

Finishing his glass of tequila, Longarm snugged down his hat, got to his feet, and walked out of the cantina.

As he paused in the doorway, the batwings flipping shut behind him, he felt the cool wind off the desert and was grateful. He moved down the street toward the hotel, approaching the first alley without hesitation, crossed before its dark, impenetrable mouth, and kept going. There were more alleys between the cantina and the hotel, and he knew that Cecil Benton would prefer one further from the cantina, away from the fitful light it shed.

The next alley offered no trouble, and only the sudden ramblings of an oversized tomcat marred the silent, black depths of the next one. Somewhat sheepishly, Longarm dropped his Colt back into its holster and continued on to the hotel. When he strode into the small lobby, he felt a little foolish. He had given Benton the opportunity he craved, and Benton had not taken it.

Either Benton had decided not to make his move now, or Longarm had been mistaken. His eyes could very well have been playing tricks on him this afternoon. That sunlight had been especially strong after the dim interior of the coach. This morbid certainty of his that Cecil Benton was preparing to fulfill a wild threat made days before in Denver could simply be the result of Longarm's overwrought nerves. After all these years, he could be losing his grip. It could happen.

He unlocked the door and stepped inside—and in that instant smelled death. He flung himself to the floor just as a double-barreled shotgun exploded in front of him. He did not see the detonation, but heard it as he kept his face down, buried in the room's threadbare carpet. The buckshot swept past his head like a wind out of hell and slammed into the wall on the other side of the hallway.

He rolled swiftly over out of the doorway, his Colt leaving his holster in one swift, fluid motion. Firing up at the man crouching behind the bed, he heard the slugs impact as they struck the wall. He fired a second time at the scurrying shadow as Benton flung himself at the window. There was the sound of glass shattering. Longarm jumped to his feet and saw Benton scramble to his feet on the porch roof outside the window, then disappear over the edge.

Longarm flung up the window sash and jumped out

onto the roof. His legs flew out from under him as he slipped on the broken shards of glass. He came down hard. Cursing bitterly, he scrambled to his feet and hurried to the edge of the roof in time to see the dark, indistinct shape of a horse and rider galloping off down the moonlit street.

He threw one futile shot after Benton, then moved back across the roof to his room. As he climbed back in through the window, he felt a little better. He had not been imagining things, after all.

It was some comfort, though not much.

Chapter 2

Above the trail following the Rio Grande, astride a broad-chested stallion, Juanita watched Longarm bid goodbye to Lieutenant Sanders and ride off. Her chestnut horse pawed uneasily as she watched Longarm disappear up the trail.

Juanita's long dark hair had been wound into a neat bun at the back of her head and the hat she wore was a high-peaked sombrero. Under her dark vest she wore a white silk blouse. A black silk bandanna was knotted about her neck. A dark woolen split skirt and riding boots, beautifully tooled, completed a riding costume that quite effectively transformed the cantina girl for whom Longarm had interceded the night before.

As soon as the lieutenant vanished from view on his

31

way back to Presidio, Juanita Lopez de Santa Rosa nudged her chestnut off the ridge and started off down the same trail Longarm had taken.

The blazing sun had been leaning heavily on him for most of the day, and Longarm was getting a mite discouraged. He could not have traveled more than twenty miles downriver, yet already the terrain was forcing him to move higher into the steep cliffs bordering its banks.

Longarm, dressed no longer in his usual outfit, now favored a black flat-crowned Stetson, Levi's, and a buttonless vest over a red-checked cotton shirt. Around his neck he had tied a red bandanna. His double-action Colt rested in a flapped holster strapped to his right thigh, and he had shoved his derringer down into his left boot where it rested not very comfortably. He had sewn his ID into his shirt tail.

He did not know what his cover story would be if and when he did manage to reach this colonel; he would think of something when the time came.

Captain Wellman had not been at all happy when he learned of Longarm's run-in with Cecil Benton the previous night. The officer made it clear to Longarm that he felt the lawman should have told him the moment he suspected Senator Benton's son was in Presidio. Wellman was certain—even if Longarm was not—that they could have set a trap for the young man and prevented the gunplay that ensued. Meanwhile, Wellman had not lost any time sending a telegram to Washington alerting the proper authorities of Cecil Benton's probable whereabouts, on the logical assumption that the senator was by this time more than a little upset by his son's disappearance from Denver. The only thing that gave Wellman any comfort was the fact that Longarm had apparently missed the young hothead when he fired on him.

But Wellman's unhappiness was of little concern to Longarm as he rode through the late-afternoon sun—especially when he became certain he was being followed.

And that the rider on his tail was Cecil Benton.

About a mile beyond the point where he first sensed he was being followed, Longarm topped a ridge, nudged his mount down the far side, then whirled about and galloped back up onto the ridge.

In that instant he caught sight of the rider following him as he passed between two fingers of rock on the trail far below. Longarm waited. When the rider failed to reappear on the other side of the rock, Longarm realized that his ploy had been caught by young Benton, who now waited behind cover for Longarm to continue. For a thoughtful moment Longarm kept his eyes on the trail, then wheeled his horse about and plunged back down the ridge.

At full gallop he continued, despite the treacherous trail, until he had reached a covey of boulders at least half a mile farther on. Some of the boulders were as big as houses. Threading his way through them, he came at last to a small, hidden clearing, dismounted, and tethered his mount to a sapling. Then, snaking his Winchester out of its scabbard, he doubled swiftly back along the trail.

He found what he was looking for after a few hundred yards—a vantage point on a ledge halfway up the slope overlooking the trail. It was so far back from the trail, Longarm was certain he would not be visible—until young Benton passed directly in front of him. Longarm pulled himself up into the rocks, came upon a smooth stove-top of cap rock and hurried across it toward the slope leading to the ledge. He had almost reached it when he heard the chink of spurs just behind him and the sound of weapons being cocked.

He turned swiftly around. The two men he had tangled with the night before were standing with guns drawn, smiles splitting their bearded faces.

"You came right to us, mister," said Jake. "Thanks."

"Come this way," said Pete. "We got someone wants to meet you."

"Paid us a pretty penny to see to it, he did," chuckled Jake. "So we wouldn't want to disappoint him none."

"Jake," said Pete, "take the son of a bitch's weapons. He won't be needin' them any more."

Jake's smell increased as he slouched nearer Longarm. On closer scrutiny, Longarm saw that his beard was a dark red, his blue eyes bloodshot, his breath—due to its whiskey content—almost combustible. Plastered to his emaciated rib cage was a faded blue cotton shirt, and the knees of his filthy Levi's were worn clean through.

Jake lifted Longarm's Colt from its holster and yanked the Winchester out of his hands. Fingering the double-action Colt, he did a quick, excited jig.

"My, oh, my!" he cried, hefting the Colt delightedly. "This here is some weapon. Yes, it is, by grannies!"

"That Colt's mine, Jake," said the other, coming up swiftly and snatching it out of Jake's hand.

"Aw, Pete! You know I need a new pistol!"

"You can have his Winchester," Pete replied, sticking Longarm's Colt into his belt and grinning at Longarm. Pete's teeth were all there, but they were black with tobacco juice.

"This way, lawman," said Pete, his head tilted to one side so that he could see Longarm more closely. "Down that trail there. You'll see some horses. Head for 'em."

Cursing himself for allowing these two to capture him so easily, Longarm moved ahead of them down the trail until he reached the horses they had tethered in a small clearing. After the two men mounted up, Jake threw a lariat about Longarm's shoulders, twisted the rope around his saddlehorn, then told Longarm to keep up. A second later, Jake spurred his mount forward with a sharp cry, and Longarm found himself running.

He fell more than once, the cruel rocks slicing into his arms and torso each time. Fortunately, they did not have far to go, and before long they pulled up on a ridge high over the Rio Grande. Waiting for them in the shadow of the cliff arching over them was young Cecil Benton.

He got to his feet as Jake yanked Longarm closer, then unwound the rope from his saddlehorn. Weary, barely able to stay on his feet, Longarm faced the senator's young son. Longarm was incredulous. How had Benton managed to get here this quickly?

"How do you feel, Long?" Benton asked, grinning. "You look kind of torn up. I hope my friends weren't too unkind."

The remark was so stupid, Longarm did not bother to answer it.

Benton walked close to Longarm and brought his right hand up quickly. The slap echoed sharply on the rocky ledge. Longarm had expected the blow. Absorbing it calmly, he lashed out with his right fist, catching Benton flush on his jaw and sending him reeling back.

Before Benton could retaliate, Pete kicked Longarm in the small of the back and sent him stumbling forward onto the hard ground. Beside himself with fury, Benton rushed over and began kicking furiously at Longarm as the big lawman pulled himself into a fetal position and hung on grimly. At last, out of breath from his violent tantrum, Benton pulled back, breathing heavily.

Longarm heard the click of a hammer and turned to look up at Benton. With a shaking hand, Benton was aiming his revolver at Longarm's head.

Longarm sat up. Benton took a nervous step back. Longarm got to his feet as slowly and as casually as he could manage under the circumstances.

"Kill me, Benton," he said calmly, "and it'll be murder. Your father already knows you made one attempt on my life last night. The commanding officer at Presidio has sent him a telegram. It would make a nice scandal, don't you think? Deputy U. S. marshal murdered by senator's son. And even if you did get away with it, these two friends of yours will have a fine time bleeding you from here on. You'll have to kill them too, looks like."

Swiftly, Benton glanced at his two partners. They backed away. Pete smiled crookedly, tipping his head and fixing Benton with his good right eye. "You don't have to worry none about us, Mr. Benton. We'll just take that money you promised us and go on our way."

"Yessir," seconded Jake hurriedly. "That's just what we'll do! Don't you worry none about us, Mr. Benton."

"I told you," said Benton, through clenched teeth. "My name is Smith."

"Oh, sure!" cried Jake eagerly. "Smith! That's right! You mustn't mind us. We just forgot when we heard this lawman call you Mr. Benton."

"He's Cecil Benton," Longarm told them. "Senator

Boris Benton's only son. You've got a powerful partner here, men. He's worth a lot of money."

"Damn you!" cried young Benton, stepping quickly back and covering both Pete and Jake along with Longarm.

"Now, listen here, Mr. Benton," said Jake. "There's no call for you to point that weapon at us."

"Don't you go listenin' to that lawman, Mr. Smith," said Pete, nervously eyeing the weapon in young Benton's hand. "Just let us take care of this hombre."

"That's just what I plan to do," said Benton.

"What do you mean?" said Jake.

"Drop your weapons, both of you. Then I'll tell you."

"Damn it, Benton!" cried Pete. "What the hell're you up to?"

"Do it!"

Glancing unhappily at each other, they reluctantly dropped their weapons to the ground and stepped back. Benton moved close and methodically tossed each weapon into the rocks above them.

"All right, you two," said Benton, smiling for the first time. "Take care of this lawman. Use your bare hands or any weapon you can devise. I'm giving this lawman here a fighting chance. And if his dead body is found, it will be obvious that he was not shot by me—that he was beaten to death by some person or persons unknown."

"But damn it," complained Jake, "he's liable to hurt us!"

"Might be. I tell you what. If only one of you survives, he will get the full amount I promised." Benton stepped back. "All right, get on with it. Punish this lawman."

Jake bent suddenly, scooped up a rock the size of his

37

fist, and hurled it at Longarm. As Longarm ducked, Pete rushed him, his head slamming hard into Longarm's chest. The force of Pete's charge sent Longarm back against a huge boulder. As Longarm struck it, Jake rushed him from the side, hooked Longarm around the neck with his arm, and, breathing hard, pulled him away from the boulder. With both Jake and Pete tugging on him, Longarm's knees gave way, and he crumpled under both men, his back slamming violently into the ground.

Lashing out desperately with his right fist, Longarm managed to catch Jake under the chin. Jake rolled back off him, clutching at his Adam's apple. Swinging up at Pete then, Longarm caught him with a hard blow to the side of his head. It rocked Pete back slightly, but he continued to straddle Longarm and began pounding him furiously about the head and shoulders.

Heaving desperately, Longarm rolled sideways and pushed himself up onto his hands and knees. Pete tried to wrestle him back to the ground, but Longarm shook him off, swung around, and caught him with a vicious punch flush on his nose. A dark gout of blood pulsed from it and Pete reeled backward, yelping. Longarm heaved himself upright. Pete, clawing blindly up at him, tried to do likewise. Longarm did not let him. He kicked him deliberately in the stomach. Pete doubled over, landed hard, then began twisting on the ground like a stomped worm.

Glancing swiftly about, Longarm saw that Benton had disappeared. For a moment there came to him the distant, fading clatter of hoofs. Swiftly, he reached into his boot for the derringer. He was pulling it free when Jake caught him from the side. Before he could bring it up, Jake

38

grabbed for the small weapon, causing it to detonate harmlessly.

Unable to brace himself, Longarm went reeling back under the force of Jake's desperate charge. Bringing the small weapon around, he managed to cock it a second time and fire. But his last round went over Jake's head as Longarm's feet flew out from under him. He came down hard on his back, a boulder embedded in the ground slamming up into the base of his skull. The inside of his head exploded as he dropped the empty weapon and fought desperately for consciousness.

Dimly, through shifting curtains of pain, he saw Jake towering over him, holding a heavy branch high over his head. With a mean grin of triumph on his face, he kicked the derringer away, then brought the branch down hard. Warding off the blow with his right forearm, Longarm rolled to one side as a second blow caught him painfully on the shoulder. He kept on rolling and heaved himself up onto his feet. Though his sudden lunge upright made it seem as if the back of his skull were hanging open, he managed to steady himself and crouch in readiness as Jake, swinging the branch murderously in front of him, slowly advanced.

As soon as Jake was close enough, Longarm flung up his arms to ward off the branch, then rushed in. He took a furious pounding about the head and shoulders before he was able to wrest the branch out of the man's grasp and fling it to one side. With a grim, murderous thoroughness, Longarm then advanced on Jake, pounding him with vicious, looping rights and lefts to his head and face, driving the man back relentlessly. In a matter of moments, Jake's knees began to sag.

Before Longarm could finish Jake off, however, Pete came at him from the side, beating him furiously with the branch Longarm had just torn from Jake's grasp. Longarm ducked away, but he was near total exhaustion by this time, and slipped to one knee as Pete continued to pound on his bowed shoulders and head. Blindly, Longarm reached down and picked up his own crude weapon—a fist-sized rock. He thrust himself up through the rain of blows and clubbed Pete viciously on the side of the head.

Stunned, Pete shook himself and staggered back. Through a curtain of red rage, Longarm kept after him. This time he brought the rock down onto the top of Pete's skull. Pete's knees buckled. He dropped the branch, but remained stubbornly on his feet. A second time Longarm slammed downward. With a muffled cry, Pete reached out for Longarm, clawing at him and bearing him to the ground with him. Rolling out from under the struggling man, Longarm struck Pete on the side of his skull, this final blow containing all he had left.

He heard the crunch of Pete's skull shattering and felt the man shudder, then grow still under him. Panting deeply, his head spinning from the incredible exertion of the past few minutes, Longarm lay with his head down over Pete's motionless body.

"Damn you to hell, mister!" came a strangled cry from above him.

Rolling over weakly, Longarm glanced up. Jake was looming over him, his face as raw as beefsteak, his puffed eyes wide in fury, a huge boulder held high over his head.

Longarm tried to summon whatever reserves his powerful body might still possess. But there was nothing left. Spent completely by the murderous intensity of this struggle, he found himself unable even to raise his hands to ward off what he knew was coming.

A rifle shot sounded clearly, sharply. Longarm heard the bullet whine off the rocks to his left and saw Jake flinch as a bloody furrow materialized along his cheekbone. That moment—that hope—was all Longarm needed. As his second wind surged through him, he rolled swiftly to one side while Jake, his knees buckling in terror, dropped the boulder and took a faltering step backward. Another rifle shot came, this one sounding still closer. In a mindless panic by this time, Jake turned to bolt.

Longarm reached out and caught Jake by the ankle. Jake thrashed frantically in an effort to pull out of Longarm's grasp, but the lawman hung on grimly and dragged Jake to the ground. Straddling his waist, he swung a hard, sledging right to Jake's chin.

Jake's head snapped around from the force of the punch. Longarm came back with a left, snapping Jake's head back the other way. In a frenzy, Jake tried to claw his way out from under Longarm, but Longarm grabbed Jake's shirtfront and hauled the man upright. A wild blood-lust surged through him now, banishing his fatigue, filling him with the joy of combat as he proceeded to punch Jake about the face and head with savage, murderous precision.

Jake backed away slowly, unable to do more than paw feebly at Longarm's ruthlessly timed punches. Blood was streaming from Jake's nose and the slice across his cheekbone made by that bullet was now a large, bloody hole

41

in the side of his face. Yet still Longarm continued to work over Jake, timing each punch, methodically measuring each crunching blow.

Whimpering now under Longarm's ceaseless, metronomic punishment, Jake finally lunged at his tormentor in a desperate, mindless attempt to escape. Longarm stepped neatly to one side. As Jake hurtled blindly past him, Longarm brought his right fist down on the man's neck, the rabbit punch dropping Jake like a poleaxed steer.

Jake landed face down and did not move. Longarm tucked his toe under Jake's belly and turned him over. Jake had come down hard on a high, sharply ridged stone embedded firmly in the ground. Its blade had punched a hole between the man's eyes, shattering the bone connecting the sockets. His lifeless eyes stared wonderingly up at Longarm.

Longarm turned the man back over onto his stomach and became aware of a sudden enormous weakness. He sagged down onto one knee, waiting for the weakness to pass. It only grew more pronounced. It was as if the universe were pushing him to the ground. He tried to stand upright, but found he had lost all power to govern his limbs. The ground shifted under his feet. He felt himself tilting backward, then falling.

When his head struck, a bolt of pain exploded deep within his skull like a cache of dynamite. Through the sudden bloody haze that clouded his vision, he saw a rider approaching. The rider was astride a magnificent chestnut and wore a high-crowned sombrero. But the eyes that looked down at him from under the sombrero's rim had tears in them, and they were the large, soft eyes of a woman.

Juanita.

It was her rifle that had saved him, then. He tried to get up, to call out to her, but darkness, like great, ominous wings, began to close about him as he watched Juanita dismount swiftly and run toward him.

The darkness reached him before she did.

Chapter 3

It was night. The first sound that came to him was that of the river far below. It filled the night air with its ceaseless mutter. He lifted his head and wished he hadn't. Groaning, he put his hand back to feel of it and found it was wrapped heavily in bandages.

"You are awake, señor?" The question came from directly behind him.

Longarm cautiously pushed himself to a sitting position and turned his head even more carefully. Sitting with her back to a boulder was the girl, Juanita. A rifle was resting across her lap.

"I'm awake, all right. How long have I been unconscious?" he asked her.

"It is close to morning, señor. For two days you rave

45

like madman. I think maybe I have to tie you down. But this night you sleep well, and you cry out no more." She leaned forward and rested her cool hand on his forehead. *"Bueno.* Now your fever, it is gone too."

"You say I've been out for two days?"

Her teeth gleamed in the darkness. "Yes, señor."

"Call me Longarm," the lawman said. "That's what my friends call me."

"I am honored that you should so regard me."

"Hell, you saved my life."

"And you saved me from those desert cockroaches."

Longarm sat up cautiously and looked around. It felt as if the loose change in his head would fall out if he wasn't very careful. "Where are they? The bodies, I mean."

With more than a trace of distaste in her voice, she replied, "I dragged them to the edge of the cliff and rolled them over. The river has them now."

Giving no indication of his surprise at her somewhat cold-blooded action, he just nodded. "It's chilly. I have some matches. Why don't we build a fire?"

"I do not think we should," she told him. "There is someone up there in the rocks watching us. I shot at him yesterday when he tried to approach. I think I hit him, but I am not certain. He wants to kill you, I am sure."

Longarm took a deep breath. Cecil Benton. That son of a bitch! He was still out there, waiting to do what his hired men could not. But now Juanita was involved and he didn't know if he liked that.

"And you shot at him, Juanita?"

"Yes. I wait for him to get close. Then I fire. But I think I am too nervous. He run very fast before he reach his horse. I send another shot after him and then he ride

46

very hard." She shuddered slightly, glancing furtively past him at the rocks that loomed about them. "But now I feel him out there in the darkness again, waiting."

"I suggest we build a fire. Then move out."

She frowned at his suggestion, but he let her think about it for a moment. Abruptly, she brightened and nodded, understanding at once what he had in mind. "I will get the firewood," she said, rising to her feet. "My horse is tethered below us on the trail, closer to the river."

"I'll need my weapons."

"I have already found them in the rocks—a Winchester, a Colt, and a whore's gun. They are beside you, wrapped in your bedroll."

"Thanks. Where's my horse?"

She shook her head sadly. "That one waiting in the rocks kill your horse. I hear the shot and when I go back to see what it is, I find the dead animal. He is such a brute, that one. After that I hurry back here to wait for him."

She left him then and in a few moments had gathered enough fuel for the campfire. Longarm lit the tinder and quickly built it into a roaring blaze. As he worked, Juanita, acting on his instructions, created two dummy sleepers using a spare saddle blanket and some deftly arranged rocks.

As quickly and as silently as they could manage in the darkness, they left the roaring campfire behind them and slipped down the rocks to Juanita's horse. Longarm found he was still too weak to ride, so they led the horse through the darkness, moving on down the river. They kept going until dawn, when they came upon a grassy sward hidden from the trail and there made a dry camp.

Longarm wanted to ask the girl what in blazes she was doing in the Big Bend country looking after his hide, but he decided it would keep; he was too exhausted. Soon he was asleep, while Juanita, at her insistence, stood guard. He awoke about midday, astonishingly refreshed and ready to devour a bear, burrs and all. Juanita produced some jerky and a full canteen of icy spring water. She had discovered the spring in the rocks above them. They ate in contented silence, after which Longarm stood guard while the girl slept.

At sundown she awoke and by this time Longarm felt strong enough to ride. He swung up in the saddle first, then pulled her up behind him. She rode astride the cantle, her arms clasped tightly around his waist. They continued down the river until well past midnight, when they halted and made camp once more.

Longarm was tired enough, but he could not sleep. He was no longer worried about Benton. They had seen no sign of him and Longarm was beginning to think Juanita's suspicion that Benton had been lurking in the rocks above them earlier was mistaken. If her account of their confrontation had been accurate, there was a good chance that her shot might well have been enough to send him back to Presidio to lick his wounds.

But it was not thoughts of Cecil Benton that kept Longarm from sleeping. He glanced to his right, then propped his head up on his elbow. His head still ached, but only slightly—a dim echo of what he had suffered earlier.

Juanita was in her own soogan less than six feet away. He could see her stirring restlessly. Longarm glanced up at the night sky. The moon had sunk out of sight behind the wall of rock that towered over them. Directly above them the stars were so incredibly clear and bright that Longarm was almost convinced that a single well-placed stone would bring down a shower of diamonds.

"Juanita," Longarm called softly.

"*Si,* señor?"

"I told you. Call me Longarm."

"*Si,* Longarm," she replied. "What is it you wish?"

"I am curious."

She turned in her soogan to face him. Her eyes seemed huge in her small face. "Curious?"

"That's right. What in tarnation are you doing in this country looking after me?"

She sat up and pushed her long black hair back off her shoulders. It gleamed in the starlight. "I come to Presidio to find someone who take me to Big Bend. Like you, I seek this crazy colonel."

Longarm was astonished. "You *what?*"

"Yes, señor, like you, I seek him."

"How in blazes did you find out about him?"

"His men take my father and brother when they stop at our ranch. And when I go to San Carlos to seek aid, no one will come with me. They say *I* am crazy. This colonel, he is very powerful man. He have army and many slaves. He and his men make the traders of Matamoros very rich. So everyone decide not to notice what he and his men do when they come through our land."

"And just what was that?"

"They do not ask for the water they take, and they do not pay for the fresh meat they devour or the horses they steal. They just take. Only my father protest because from him they take so much. When one of their men try to take me, he go after that soldier with rifle, and I run away into the rocks and hide. I look back and see what

49

happen then. Many soldiers take my father's rifle from him. They beat him. My brother, Pepe, try to stop them, so they beat him too. And when the soldiers ride off, they take them both."

"Was this their usual behavior, Juanita?"

She shook her head sadly. "No. Most times they just take water and food and move on. But this time the captain in charge of the freight wagons was very drunk, too drunk to control his men. That is why it happened, I think."

"You went to San Carlos then?"

"Yes. But when I find no one will help, I cross the river and ride north to Presidio. There I work for my uncle in his cantina. While I am there I ask some soldiers to help me, but they only laugh. I have no home now, so I stay at cantina with my uncle. Then when the captain come back and die, there is much talk, and I hear a man such as you will come soon. So I wait."

"You say you heard about me? From whom?"

She hesitated only an instant. "From Lieutenant Sanders. He is my good friend. But he does not know how closely I listen to his words. He think I am one of those who do not believe there is such a canyon. So he speaks freely."

"What was your plan? To stay on my tail and follow me to the canyon?"

"Yes."

"It was you I saw tailing me then. I thought it was Benton."

"I am not so good at following a rider without he see me. That is true."

"Tell me about the colonel. Have you ever seen him?"

"No. No one sees him. But his soldiers we see, many

times, as they ride by on their way to Matamoros. Some say in their wagons is much cotton and opium. I believe it. When my father and I see a wagon overturn, the soldiers warn us to tell no one what we see."

"And what *did* you see?"

"Cotton. Many bales."

"Do you know which canyon they headed for?"

She shook her head. "It is north of the Rio Grande, past the Canyon of the Little Mouths, I think. Once my father heard the soldiers talking."

"How far from that canyon are we?"

"It is two, maybe three days' ride past Comanche Crossing, I think. But the trail the soldiers take is hidden. Many *rurales* have crossed the Rio Grande in search of it. But each time they come back with nothing. I know because they stop at my father's ranch in their unhappiness. At such times we must feed their bellies to make them happy again." She looked hopefully at Longarm. "But now you come. You know where is this hidden canyon and this crazy colonel, and you will take me with you. Is that not so?"

Longarm lay back down. He did not have the heart to tell her how little he knew of the canyon's location. "We'll start in the morning," he told her.

"*Bueno.*" She was still looking at him. He could feel her large eyes watching him. After a while she said, "Longarm?"

"Yes?"

She hesitated a moment, then, in a barely audible voice, said, "When you save me from those two cockroaches, you were not saving the honor of a virgin, señor."

"That's not important, Juanita. What mattered was

51

that you didn't want to go with those two men."

Her voice still soft, she asked, "Do you not wish to know why I speak of this now?"

He turned his head to look at her. "Maybe you better tell me."

"I . . . cannot say any more. A . . . true gentleman would not ask me to do so . . ."

"My apologies," Longarm said softly. Then he smiled. "I think I understand. It was that long ride . . . with your arms about my waist. The closeness . . ."

Her eyes brightened in gratitude. "Yes," she cried, "it was that! Oh, Longarm! I think I die if you do not take me!"

Longarm needed no further urging. He flipped open his soogan. "Get in here," he told her, his voice suddenly husky with desire.

She was out of her soogan and beside him in an instant, fitting her long, unashamedly naked body close against his. It fit like a warm, silken sheath. He kissed her, not on the lips, but on the neck, under her ear. She sighed as he gently moved his lips up to nibble on one of her earlobes.

He was teasing her deliberately, aware of the passion building within her. He let his hand explore the warmth of her breasts, his fingers flicking the upraised nipples delicately. She began to groan.

Only then did he take her lips in his. They softened, opened for his probing tongue, the sweet scent of her coming to him, inflaming him. Her hands had already found his erection. Feverishly, she stroked him. He had not had a woman in too long, he realized, and would not be able to prolong his play with her, and that was a shame.

He grabbed her hip and pulled her hard against him. Without hesitation, she raised her leg for him. He thrust upward and flowed effortlessly into her warmth. Sighing, she dropped her leg and seemed to suck him deep into her. Then she began to move with a measured slowness, continuing to sigh every now and then. Longarm lay still, content to feel her inner pulsing wrapping him in soft sensation.

Juanita shuddered gently, relaxed, and lay motionless for several minutes. Then she began to move again, this time with a slow rotation of her hips. Almost imperceptibly, Longarm eased himself up onto her. She dug her heels into his back and continued to rotate her hips until another shudder passed through her, quicker this time than before.

As she lay back, her eyes closed, a flush Longarm could see even in the moonless darkness suffused her face. He grasped her breast, its firm, silken smoothness alive under his palm. In a moment her nipple was rock-hard. Cupping his hand gently, he moved it to her other breast and began to caress it also. Juanita began to quiver. She opened her eyes and stared up at him.

"Go deep, Longarm!" she cried.

He lunged into her swiftly and fiercely, exulting in her cry of pleasure. Arching his back above her, he pushed hard, driving deep, the flood building in him, forcing him to speed, to thrust, until it crested and burst and Juanita's cries faded to a long, sobbing moan, and then to silence.

Longarm relaxed, lying heavily on top of her, too spent to move. She bore his weight with a little murmur of satisfaction. In the starlight, her eyes gleamed with the pleasure he had given her. She smiled, reached her

53

arms up and pulled him closer upon her breasts, caressing his moist hair, murmuring softly to him, her lips moving gently, lovingly, over his forehead and face.

"You make me feel so good, Longarm. Thank you. You do not think me bad woman?"

"You make me feel just as good, Juanita. I don't think you should worry about good and bad. A man and a woman together is the most natural thing in the world. Maybe the best."

"But I am so shameless!"

"You mean passionate. Let's not question what we are, Juanita. Let us just take advantage of it and enjoy it."

"Yes, my Longarm. Yes. You are a true gentleman."

They spoke no more. He rolled gently off her and pulled her close, his lips fastened to hers while he stroked her back and thighs, exploring occasionally the moist warmth of her pubis. She returned his caresses with her own, no less effective; and before long, he came alive once more and found himself thrusting urgently toward her. Laughing gently in triumph, she pushed him over onto his back and swiftly mounted him.

He grinned up at her as she impaled herself eagerly upon his shaft, then leaned far back, a deep sigh escaping from her. With a quick toss of her head, she sent her long dark tresses back off her shoulder. Looking up at her face through the cleft of her arching breasts, he thought he had never seen anything more beautiful. At first Juanita used only her pelvic muscles, but then she began to rock. He closed his eyes and leaned back, doing all he could to hold off while she built to her climax. But soon it became apparent he was not going to be able to hold back any longer. He began to cry out.

Sensing his need, she panted, "It is fine, Longarm! I come now! I am ready!"

In grateful response, his big hands grabbed her pelvic bones. Crushing her down onto his erection, he drove himself still deeper into her, then thrust upward so violently he nearly threw her off him. Her head arching back, her fingers digging into his forearms, they both climaxed, he groaning in relief, she gasping and uttering tiny, happy shouts, like a little girl who has just been given a present.

She fell forward onto him, her face buried deliciously in the cavity between his head and shoulder. He wrapped his arms about her, pressing her breasts against him, feeling the supple warmth of her body, aware of the sweet scent of her breath on his neck.

She did not move back to her own soogan that night.

By the time they had journeyed two full days beyond Comanche Crossing, it became obvious to Longarm that they could no longer follow the river from the shore. Precipitous cliffs bordered the river, which had now become a roaring millrace white with rapids and puckered with innumerable whirlpools. Meanwhile, the only trail their horse was able to negotiate continued to lead them farther and farther away from the river. At last, on Juanita's suggestion, they moved inland to a friendly settlement where she had a distant relative. There they replenished their supplies, bought an axe, then left Juanita's horse with her relative and returned to the river.

In less than two days Longarm had lashed together a sturdy raft of cottonwood logs, stored their goods in the center, and on a bright, cloudless morning poled out into the flood of brown gravy, while Juanita manned the crude tiller he had fashioned from a branch. As the current took the raft, Longarm looked back and thought he caught a glimpse of a familiar rider peering down from the crest of a towering bluff. Before Longarm could study the figure more closely, the raft swept around a bend, and he found he had all he could do to keep it in the center of the swift channel. Glancing back at Juanita, he had sudden misgivings.

She was wearing Levi's and a man's shirt and had tied her hair back with a black ribbon. Grimly aware of what might lie ahead of them both, he hoped the ribbon's color did not prove appropriate.

Juanita caught his glance. "Do not worry about me, Longarm," she told him. "I swim like a fish. This river, it have no terror for me."

"Well, it sure as hell worries me some."

She laughed. "It will be all right. And see how fast we go! It is much better than riding, is it not?"

"That remains to be seen."

A sandbar stopped them a little after noon, and they took advantage of it to drag the raft closer to the shore and fill their bellies. The sourdough, beans, and jerky went well with the coffee she insisted on preparing. And he had to admit, she knew how to make coffee that would stick to a man's ribs.

Longarm could have lain on the cool sand for the rest of that day. His head still bothered him some, and from the moment he had begun to pole the raft, he realized that Benton's two hired assassins had done quite a job on his rib cage and lower back. He realized now why, earlier that morning, Juanita had remarked with some awe on the multicolored abundance of bruises covering his torso.

But Juanita was anxious to move on. Though she had not told him very much, what she did tell Longarm about her father and brother conveyed her deep concern for them. He did not protest, then, when she urged him to break camp and helped him push the raft out into the water on the other side of the sandbar.

As he scrambled onto it and snatched up his pole, he glanced at Juanita. There was a very determined look on her face—and no trace of fear at all at what might lie ahead.

Longarm could only admire Juanita's grit, and was determined to equal it. Still, he was not sure that she had a proper respect for this land's awesome, unforgiving savagery. They were sweeping through the Chisos Mountains now, and great peaks and towering mesas dominated the range. Canyon walls loomed almost straight up for hundreds of yards. Gorges seemed to have been sliced out of tablelands by giant meat cleavers. The Almighty could well have forgotten this place, Longarm realized, but he sure as hell must have played here for a while before moving on. Intimidating though this bleak, rugged country was, Longarm was unable to deny its rugged grandeur.

At the same time, he found it difficult, if not impossible, to believe that the U. S. Cavalry had just succeeded in flushing Victorio and his Apache band from this country. And he found it easy to understand how a mad colonel from the Confederacy might well have been able to establish his own kingdom within this uncharted, canyon-pocked wilderness.

Less than a couple of miles away, the raft swept around a bend and Longarm saw looming suddenly, massively ahead of them a great mesa through which the river sliced. They were more than a quarter of a mile from the entrance to the canyon, but even at that distance Longarm could hear the water's dim roar. He glanced at Juanita. She, too, was staring at the dark mouth of the canyon.

Soon, Longarm felt the raft begin to surge under him. As the current quickened, the river became almost as smooth as glass. The roar from the canyon increased. He glanced again at Juanita and shouted to her to hang on to that tiller. She nodded quickly.

As he swept still closer to the canyon, he glimpsed its walls. They appeared to shoot straight up for hundreds of feet. The roar grew intimidating the moment they swept into the canyon. A cool, threatening darkness fell over them. Glancing up at the sheer walls, Longarm saw the blue sky disappear into a long, distant slit. They might as well be thundering into the bowels of hell, he thought to himself grimly as the raft's speed picked up ominously.

The water's continuous roar made any conversation between him and Juanita impossible as she clung stubbornly to the crude tiller while he hopped about with his pole, doing his best to keep the raft in the center of the channel and away from the granite cliffs that swept by with such awesome speed.

A sudden roar, greater than any he had heard so far, caused him to look swiftly back at the river ahead.

They were sweeping around a shoulder of rock. For a moment it appeared that the raft was going to start spinning helplessly, but between them they managed to keep it steady on course. Then Longarm saw the white water ahead of them and groaned. The river was being squeezed through a narrow bottleneck.

Somehow they would have to keep the raft in the center. If they just grazed either side, Longarm was certain the raft would break up on the instant. He glanced back at Juanita. Her dark eyes were wide as she saw what lay ahead.

"Steady as she goes!" he shouted.

She nodded grimly, hugging the tiller to her.

He hurried to the front of the raft and poised himself carefully, ready to scramble in either direction. When the raft began to sweep toward the wall on Longarm's right, he stepped to that side and began poling frantically in an effort to push the raft away. He succeeded for a while, but the current was too strong. The raft and its two occupants bobbed about like a cork in a maelstrom.

Abruptly, the raft began to turn. He felt the pole being torn from his grasp and was almost flung with it into the boiling water. He looked back at Juanita and saw her holding what was left of the rudder, her eyes wide in sudden terror as she stared up at the onrushing canyon wall.

The raft struck. To his astonishment, it did not break up. Instead, it cartwheeled, sending them and their provisions flying. As they were flung into the roaring water, the raft slapped back down onto the slick surface of the water and swept ahead of them through the canyon.

Longarm searched the water for Juanita. When he saw her, he tried to swim in her direction, but found it impossible to buck the current. She waved to him and he thought he heard her cry out something encouraging as she was flung on past him.

Longarm had all he could do to keep afloat. His boots had filled with water and were like lead weights pulling him inexorably down. He tried unsuccessfully to kick them off, then gave it up as a bad job and began to swim frantically. He was almost through the canyon when he spied a log bearing down on him. He ducked just in time. The log swept past him, and when he surfaced a moment later he was beyond the mesa, the river spreading flat and calm before him—once again a river and not a destructive torrent.

Juanita was standing on the left shore. When she caught sight of him, she waded out waist-high, waving to him. Grimly, he struck out for her. She had not underestimated her ability to take care of herself, it appeared, and seemed almost as much at home in these unruly waters as was the flotsam the river swept along in its grasp.

They found their single bundle of provisions, which Longarm had carefully wrapped in his oilskin slicker, a few miles down the river in the shallows. Not long after that, they came upon the raft wedged firmly into a sandbar. The flour and coffee were ruined, but the beef jerky was still edible, and the cans of beans were battered but intact.

Longarm's weapons needed careful cleaning and he took considerable time checking his ammunition. They made camp that night in a cottonwood grove, where Longarm turned his attention to the condition of his raft. It was still in one piece, but slamming into that wall and the subsequent rush through the canyon had loosened the logs. Longarm spent the rest of the evening taking the raft apart and lashing it together again.

Less than an hour after starting out the next morning, they came to a rock fall that effectively blocked the channel ahead of them. The river tumbled through and over the rocks swiftly enough, but it took Longarm and Juanita the rest of the day to haul the raft and their belongings over the barrier. They camped on the shore on the other side of it just before sundown. Longarm estimated that they could not have covered more than two, or at the most, three miles that day. Juanita was very discouraged.

They swept past Boquillas Canyon—the Canyon of the Little Mouths, as Juanita called it—the next day, a little before noon. The captain had suggested this canyon as a possible site for the colonel's enterprise, since it was the largest and most inaccessible of the Big Bend's canyons. But Longarm remembered something from Miles Winthrop's account, and had mentioned it to Juanita. Winthrop had described the canyon as having a very broad entrance, marked by a tall, sentinel-like finger of rock. The entrance to Boquillas Canyon was quite narrow and there was no rock formation near its entrance that remotely resembled a sentinel.

As they left Boquillas Canyon behind them, the water quickened markedly, and soon Longarm found himself scrambling to avoid a series of huge rocks that loomed suddenly up before them like the petrified effigies of ancient sea monsters. But somehow, by dint of furious poling and a lot of tugging on the tiller on Juanita's part, they were able to sweep past them and continue on to a wide, meandering stretch of the river as it cut through a broad valley that appeared to stretch before them for miles.

For close to an hour they continued, talking amiably to each other, while they remarked on the peaks that soon began to loom on all sides of them. These were the Chisos Mountains, sharply peaked humps that seemed to rise with precipitate haste into the iron-blue sky.

Longarm was still caught up in a rapt appreciation of the spectacular landscape when he felt the raft's pace quicken. He turned his attention to the channel ahead of him and saw that the raft was approaching a bend in the river that took them between two towering mesas. As they got closer to the mesas, he heard the roar of fast water. Their brief respite was coming to an end.

He glanced back at Juanita. She too had heard the deep mutter and was clutching the tiller a little more closely.

They swept around the bend. Sheer cliffs closed about the river channel. The light from the sky diminished. At that moment Longarm saw, at least a quarter of a mile further on, the mouth of a wide canyon where it emptied into the river. And on the far side of the canyon's mouth a tall finger of rock stood—like a sentinel.

Longarm shouted to Juanita and pointed at the marker. "There it is!" he cried.

She had seen it also and nodded eagerly.

The raft swept on. The roaring sound ahead of them increased. Peering through the misty netherworld, Longarm was astonished to see what he thought was smoke coming up from the surface of the river close to the far wall of the canyon. As the raft surged closer, he kept his eye on the spot. And then, as he realized what lay before them, he felt the hair on the back of his neck rise.

As the river charged on past the canyon entrance, it piled up against its far wall, then spun about and flung itself on past with such force that it created an enormous, surging whirlpool. Longarm was just barely able to glimpse the sweeping rim that formed at the edge of the maelstrom and above it the light spray that drifted like smoke over the swirling vortex.

As if that were not enough, Longarm remembered what Winthrop had told the captain: beyond the entrance to this canyon there were murderous rapids, the same rapids that had chewed him up so fearfully. Finding the canyon, it seemed, had been the easy part. Getting off this raft and entering the canyon in one piece was evidently going to be something else again.

Longarm looked back at Juanita. "There's a whirlpool ahead of us," he shouted, leaning close so she could hear him. "Steer away from the canyon and keep to the other side of the channel. We'll have to take our chances in the rapids beyond."

Juanita nodded grimly, smiled uncertainly up at him, and then began to lean all her weight on the tiller. Longarm positioned himself on the edge of the raft and began poling furiously. Luckily, he found subsurface rocks substantial enough to push off of, and the raft began edging toward the far side of the channel.

They were almost abreast of the maelstrom when Longarm felt the raft being tugged toward it. Redoubling his efforts, he poled furiously, and a moment later the pull of the whirlpool lessened as they swept beyond its influence. The raft was caught in the outflow from the whirlpool, and with breathtaking speed was swept past the canyon's entrance and around a sharp bend.

The rapids were upon them before they could react. A black rock loomed directly ahead. Juanita leaned on the tiller as Longarm raced up to fend off the towering obstruction. But the raft struck the rock headlong. With a fierce crack, it split down the middle, flinging Longarm and Juanita backward into the roaring waters. Avoiding the leaping, splintering raft, Longarm pulled through the seething waters, aware of Juanita's bobbing head a few feet in front of him as she struck out for the shore.

But the current was too swift to allow much control. A rock slammed into Longarm's chest. When he reached out to grab it, he was flung past it. He felt himself turning as he was sucked under the surface. He tried to regain it, but as he did, something struck him a numbing blow on the side of the head. Blinking to clear his senses, he continued to pull blindly for the surface and broke through in a patch of swift but unobstructed waters. He saw Juanita paddling feebly just ahead of him, her face down in the water.

He swam swiftly to her side and caught her under the arms, turning her over so that her face was out of the water, then struck out for a flat rock closer to the shore. When he reached it, he pushed her up onto it. As soon as she was secure, he reached up and slapped her to make sure she was all right. She opened her eyes and smiled weakly at him. The sight cheered him immensely.

Feeling for all the world like some monstrous species of drowned rat, he started to pull himself up after her. They could both try to make it to the shore later, he told himself, after they had regained their strength. As he was pulling himself onto the rock, he saw a tiny geyser erupt in the water behind him. A second later, a ricocheting bullet took a chunk out of the rock inches from his right hand.

Grabbing Juanita roughly, he pushed her back into the water, then tumbled in after her, paddling with her to the side of the rock farthest from the shore. Above the infernal, constant roar of the rapids, he could not hear the gunfire, but there was no doubt about it. Someone on shore was shooting at them.

Chapter 4

"Stay down," Longarm told the confused Juanita. "Some-one is firing at us."

A bullet ricocheted off the surface of the rock only inches above her head. As the tiny shards of pulverized rock peppered her face, she gasped and shrank still further down into the water, staring wild-eyed at Longarm as she did so. She had been totally exhausted a moment before. Now she was close to panic.

"It's probably young Benton," he told her. "Keep down."

She nodded uncertainly as another bullet ricocheted off the rock. This time, Longarm thought he heard the rifle shot above the roar of the water. It had come from the rocks on the canyon side.

Longarm peered around the rock and tried to pick out some movement along the shore. A scurrying figure, perhaps, or the gleam of sunlight on a rifle barrel. Despite what he had just told Juanita, however, he did not expect to see Benton. He had only suggested Benton might be the culprit in order to calm her. Because she had already dealt with him once, his hope was that she would not have as great a fear of him as she would of someone else. But there was little chance Benton could have kept up with their raft, since there was no trail that followed the river close enough to bring him this far, this soon— as both the lieutenant and Captain Wellman had been at some pains to point out.

As he poked his head out around the rock, hoping for some glimpse of whoever was firing on them, a tiny geyser of water shot up inches from his head and he heard the rifle's report. Peering at the rocks, he saw movement, and then a swift figure running across an open space.

In that single glimpse, he saw what he was up against—and wished that it had been Benton after all. The running figure had long hair and was wearing a breechcloth. Apaches.

"What is it?" Juanita asked him as he ducked his head back behind the rock. "Did you see who is shooting at us? Is it Benton?"

"I saw someone," he said, "but he was too far away for me to be sure if it was Benton or not."

"What are we going to do?" she asked.

"Hang on until it gets dark. Then we can swim to shore and I'll see what I can do about that fellow. Right now he's got us pinned good and proper."

Longarm glanced up at the sky. Nightfall was hours

away. He wondered if they would be able to hang on to this rock for that long. He swam closer to Juanita. She was shivering and he could hear her teeth chattering. He pressed his body against hers and she leaned gratefully back against him. This seemed to help some, as the warmth of their bodies combined.

Only an occasional shot came now to remind them that they were still under fire. Doing his best to ignore the shots, Longarm clung to the rock and did what he could to comfort Juanita as the swift, unheeding waters of the Rio Grande swept past.

As soon as it was dark enough, they left the rock and swam underwater for some distance down the river, then struck out for the shore. It was not so easy as it had appeared, since the river's current was exceedingly strong, but they managed to pull themselves free of it and floundered ashore.

As soon as they found shelter in the rocks, Longarm told Juanita to stay low while he doubled back along the shore to see to that son of a bitch who had been firing on them. She clung to him for a moment, unwilling to let him go, but he extricated himself gently and set off. Longarm was unarmed, but he was hoping surprise and the darkness would make up for this weakness.

It was not long before he heard movement in the rocks ahead of him. Ducking back, he waited alertly as the light pat of Apache moccasins slapping the ground grew closer. There was more than one pair of moccasins. Longarm drew further back into the shadows and kept low.

There were two of them. The first Apache did not carry a rifle; the second one did. Reaching out swiftly,

Longarm snatched the rifle away from the second savage. The Indian spun around just as Longarm swung the rifle like a club, catching the savage on the side of his head. The Apache crumpled to the ground as his companion, momentarily transfixed, crouched low and prepared to rush Longarm. Longarm levered the Winchester and aimed it coolly at the second Apache's midsection. The Apache halted, straightened slowly, and took a step back.

He was an odd Apache, indeed, Longarm commented to himself—far taller and more rangy than the average. And he had eyes that were much too light. Longarm was willing to bet that if the sun were out, he would find himself looking into a blue-eyed Apache.

Still covering the Indian, Longarm went down on one knee and nudged over the one he had clubbed unconscious and looked into his face. He was not surprised to find himself looking at another well-tanned but indubitably white "Apache."

"They were too damned careless," said a cold voice from behind Longarm. "You should have killed them."

Longarm spun. Something sharp and unyielding struck him on the chin, slamming him brutally back. His heel caught a root and he fell heavily, his head spinning.

It was difficult to see clearly, but Longarm appeared to be facing a small army patrol—a Confederate Army patrol, judging from the uniforms—consisting of four enlisted men and one officer. The officer was a lieutenant, and it was he who had spoken and who had struck Longarm with the butt of his revolver.

Groggily, Longarm felt his chin and tried to calm his rage. He pushed himself upright slowly. "Who in blazes are you?" he demanded.

"Your servant, sir. Lieutenant Dumas Tyler."

"Do you mind telling me what in hell is going on

here, Lieutenant? A masquerade ball, maybe—with men disguised as Apaches and Confederate soldiers."

He ignored Longarm's outburst. "Your name, sir?"

"Will Montana."

The lieutenant smiled coldly. "And what in hell are you doing on this river, Mr. Montana? Don't you know what a treacherous course it follows through these mountains?"

Grudgingly, Longarm nodded. "I do now, damn it! If I'd'a known it was going to turn out as wet as this, I would have stuck to my horse."

"And where were you heading?"

"Del Rio. Some fool of a drunk told me I could get there from El Paso by following the Rio Grande through these mountains. I guess maybe I was in too much of a hurry to get out of El Paso to find out what I was gettin' into."

"The law is after you, is it?"

"You might say that."

"And where is the woman who was with you on that raft? Did she survive?"

"She survived, all right. I left her downstream."

"Take us to her. The colonel will want to see you both, I am sure. That woman of yours, especially." Longarm thought he caught a note of bitterness in the lieutenant's tone.

The lieutenant nodded to Longarm, indicating that he should precede them down the trail. Longarm turned and made his way through the darkness ahead of them. Detailing a man to stay with the still groggy "Apache" Longarm had knocked unconscious, the lieutenant and the rest of his party filed along behind the lawman. There was no further conversation.

Longarm found the spot where he had left Juanita

without too much difficulty, but there was no sign of the girl. He stopped, puzzled, and looked around, his eyes searching the dark rocks for some sign of her.

The lieutenant halted beside him. "Where is she?" he asked.

"I left her here. But she's nowhere around, looks like."

The lieutenant's eyes narrowed. "Are you sure this is where you left her?"

"Hell, if you don't believe me, look at these tracks. We made enough when we came ashore."

"Call to her. She heard us coming and is hiding in the rocks, more than likely."

"Juanita!" he called. "You out there? It's Will!"

There was no response, just the faint echo of his words among the rocks and the dim mutter of the river. He called out one more time, then turned to the lieutenant. "She lit out, looks like. A real spunky wench, that one." Longarm grinned at the officer. "Guess maybe this here colonel of yours will have to find his own woman."

The lieutenant turned to his men. "Spread out! Find her! She's around here somewhere."

But she wasn't.

An hour later the lieutenant and his soldiers were high above the Rio Grande, leading Longarm along a ridge that ran parallel to the canyon Longarm and Juanita had risked so much to find.

Peering down at the canyon floor, Longarm could see no end to it. The canyon could easily extend for twenty or thirty miles, he realized. The moon had risen by this time, and Longarm was able to glimpse the sheer cliffs that hemmed in the valley as well as the irrigated fields

70

below. Each neat, almost geometrically perfect field was outlined in silver as the irrigated ditches bordering them reflected the moonlight.

To reach the canyon floor, they descended by a wide, steep trail that appeared to have been hacked and dynamited out of the cliff wall by a stupendous effort of manual labor that must have taken a considerable time. It was close to dawn when Longarm and his captors reached the valley floor and marched through a settlement that had been built close in under the protective overhang of the cliff they had just descended. The town appeared to be a thriving community, including a saloon, a general store, a blacksmith shop, and a feed and grist mill built over a narrow stream.

As they marched down the silent street, a tall woman stepped out onto the second-floor balcony of the town's cathouse. It was newly whitewashed and in excellent repair.

"Hey there, Lieutenant!" the woman called down. "Ain't it late for you boys to be out?"

"Not a bit of it, Samantha!" the lieutenant yelled up to her. "What's the matter? A quiet night?"

The woman laughed. She had flaming red hair that flowed down the back of her scarlet nightgown, which she wore off her ivory shoulders, shamelessly. She must have been drinking, Longarm surmised, judging from the way she slurred her words.

"Who you got there?" she demanded. "A new recruit? We get first crack at him, remember!"

"Don't worry, you will," the lieutenant replied as they kept on over a wooden bridge on their way out of the town.

Not long after, Longarm caught sight of an impressive

mansion complete with massive white pillars fronting it and a broad veranda with a balcony extending the full length of the house. There was even a winding driveway through an aisle of cottonwoods leading up to the house.

There was no doubt in Longarm's mind that this was the colonel's residence.

Longarm's captors kept him moving and, at last, on a distant flat well beyond the mansion, they marched onto a military post made up of low, solidly built bunk-houses facing a small parade ground. On a flagpole in front of the headquarters building the Confederate flag hung slackly in the cool night air.

A chill ran up Longarm's back. It was fifteen years since the War Between the States had ended, yet here was a Confederate outpost—as solid and as real as the grit in his boots.

Longarm was led to an adobe guardhouse behind the headquarters building. He was its only guest. As the lieutenant slammed the cell door shut on Longarm, he drawled, "You'll probably see the colonel before your court-martial, first thing in the morning."

"Court-martial? For what?"

"You assaulted one of our men."

"Don't you feel a little silly, Lieutenant? The War's over, you know."

The lieutenant shrugged. "Maybe for you. Not for us." He turned wearily about and left the guardhouse.

Longarm stood by the window and watched the lieutenant and his men move off, shaking his head in disbelief. He thought he had been prepared to accept this mad colonel's world when he first discussed it with Billy Vail and later with Captain Wellman. But now he wanted to grab those soldiers and shout into their faces that the

War was over—that the South had lost and the Union had been saved. They could go home.

But of course that was the madness of it. For most of these young soldiers, they were already home. This world was all they knew—and this colonel the only law they had to follow.

Longarm slumped down onto the bunk and closed his eyes. He should have been too upset to sleep, and for a moment he found himself wondering what had happened to Juanita. But that painful concern was all he remembered as, totally exhausted, he sank almost at once into a deep, dreamless sleep.

Longarm was being shaken roughly by a private in the Confederate Army.

Blinking, he sat up. A tin pie plate containing his breakfast was in the young lad's hand. He put it down on a small table by the bed and stepped back, his pale blue eyes regarding Longarm curiously.

Longarm picked up the plate and stared at it. Scrambled eggs and beans, with a tin cup of hot black coffee to wash it down. He ate gratefully and, when he had finished, handed the plate and cup back to the private.

"What's your name?" Longarm asked.

"Private Scofield, sir."

"How long you been in the army, Scofield?"

The private frowned earnestly as he considered the question. "As long as I can remember, sir."

"Did you know that the War is over, Private?"

"That's what some people say, I reckon. But I don't much believe that. The colonel will tell us when it's over. Besides, we got it pretty nice and peaceful here."

"Except when strangers like me wander in."

"Guess that's so, sir."

"Any orders for me, Private Scofield?" Longarm asked wearily.

"No, sir. But I reckon you'll be having an escort to the big house soon enough."

He stepped out of the cell, closed the door, and locked it. Then, without a glance back, he vanished through the outer door.

A few minutes later, Longarm heard the heavy tramp of an army detail halting outside the guardhouse. There was a sharp command followed by the clatter of a saber and a jingle of keys as a lieutenant and two enlisted men entered the guardhouse, opened the door to Longarm's cell, and escorted him out into the brilliant sunshine of the early morning.

The lieutenant was older than Longarm by at least ten years and seemed decidedly out of sorts. The detail he commanded consisted of four privates, all as young as the hairless youth who had brought Longarm his breakfast. With weary precision, the lieutenant gave his orders, and they marched off through the bright morning.

Before long, the big house—as Private Scofield called it—was visible in the distance. In the clear morning sunlight, perched atop its gentle rise, the impressive two-story mansion appeared to be bathed in light. In spite of himself, Longarm was impressed.

But even more impressive than the colonel's mansion was the activity that greeted the new day. Longarm saw the hurrying figures of the colonel's slaves everywhere. The women, wearing long, colorful dresses and with their heads wrapped in snow-white turbans, were hurrying either toward the town or the military compound with empty wicker baskets balanced on their heads. Others were busy lugging oversized wooden tubs filled with clothing toward a large canal Longarm had not noticed the night before, but which appeared to run the length of the valley.

On the other side of the canal, slaves were busy pushing wagons piled high with cotton, or pulling empty wagons toward the cotton fields. In the fields themselves, Longarm glimpsed the bobbing, obedient heads of the slaves bent over rows of cotton that extended as far as the eye could see.

When they reached the colonel's mansion, Longarm realized that his coming had been heralded. Loitering on the porch, obviously in order to get a glimpse of this strange outsider, were four curious young men and women. The two women were dressed in a florid, wasp-waisted style that would have been appropriate twenty years before, and their dandified escorts were wearing suits just as outdated. One of the women held a parasol and twirled it excitedly as Longarm mounted the veranda steps. She had long auburn tresses and eyes that flashed with mischief. All four seemed delighted at Longarm's appearance, and the coquettish glances from the women as Longarm was escorted past them were surprisingly bold and provocative.

Inside, the colonel was waiting for Longarm in his study, behind an enormous desk. The study was book-lined and sumptuous, the furniture richly upholstered. A massive fireplace filled the far wall. Over the mantelpiece hung a large oil portrait of the colonel in full battle regalia astride a magnificent white stallion. The colonel was brandishing his gleaming saber, and behind him a battlefield was in full eruption with brooding clouds close overhead. Behind the desk, the heavy, wine-colored drapes were drawn across the French doors to prevent the brilliant morning sunlight from blinding those within.

The colonel dismissed Longarm's escort with a curt nod, then looked coldly at Longarm. "I am Colonel Bascom Sutpen, sir. I wish I could say it was a pleasure to welcome you."

"Name's Will Montana," Longarm replied.

"Sit down, Montana," the colonel said, indicating an easy chair beside his desk. As he spoke, he took a cheroot out of a small humidor and offered it to Longarm.

Longarm took it warily. Could this man possibly know who he really was? The colonel passed him a match, then lit his own smoke. Puffing on his cheroot, the colonel sat back down in his chair, regarding Longarm reflectively. Lighting up himself, Longarm studied the colonel just as intently.

Colonel Sutpen was as impressive as his portrait. A ruggedly handsome, clean-shaven man in his late fifties or early sixties, he had a high forehead, a powerful hooked beak of a nose, and a chin that seemed hewn out of granite. All of it was framed in a magnificent halo of gleaming, snow-white hair. He was wearing a white linen suit over a white broadcloth shirt, and a black string tie was at his throat.

The colonel glanced at a report that had been placed before him on his desk and frowned slightly. "I understand you injured one of my men last night."

"I should have killed him," Longarm said. "He and that other false Apache with him were trying to kill me. Was that your idea, Colonel? Dressing them two up like Apaches?"

The colonel nodded. "Their function—as I am sure

76

you have guessed—was to serve as an early warning, their gunfire alerting us to the fact that strangers were on the river. At times in the past, of course, they have managed not only to warn us but also to dispose of the threat as well. And whatever hardy souls managed to survive their hostile welcome would be able to relate only that they had been attacked by Apaches."

"You going to court-martial me, Colonel?"

"For assaulting one of my men?"

"I was told that would be the charge."

The colonel looked shrewdly at Longarm. "That would be the usual course, Mr. Montana. However, I may have other plans for you. Lieutenant Tyler's report mentions that you are a fugitive from Yankee justice."

"Guess you might call it that. I had to punish a gambler I found dealing from the bottom of the deck."

"I see nothing reprehensible in that."

"Neither did I. But his brother did, and he was the sheriff."

"I see." The colonel smiled thinly. "There were reports that you had a companion with you on that raft. A woman, I believe."

"She was that, all right. But I don't know where she is now. Somewhere down the river, maybe."

"A Mexican wench?"

"Yes."

The colonel smiled. "Too bad she got away."

"What are you going to do with me, Colonel?"

"I'm not sure." He frowned. "As you will see if you look closely about you, our outpost needs older, more solid recruits. Our women are doing their best, Mr. Montana, but they have not been able to supply this dwindling command with the number and quality of recruits we require. It is a shame. We need men. Men like you—soldily built, aggressive, in their prime—men who are not afraid to act. I must admit I was impressed by Lieutenant Tyler's report, which described in some detail not only your skill in surviving the river, but in ringing the bell of one of our toughest lookouts."

"You're thinking of asking me to join this command of yours?"

"Does that surprise you, Mr. Montana?"

"Now, let's just eat this here apple one bite at a time. You mean you're still recruiting soldiers for the War?"

The colonel smiled wearily. "My dear sir, of course not."

"Then you do know it's over."

The colonel nodded grimly. "We know the War is over, that the Yankees have won, and that for the past fifteen years the Union has been consolidating its stranglehold over our Confederate States. For thirteen years now we have been trading with Mexican merchants in Matamoros. It would have been impossible for our men not to have learned during this long intercourse with the citizens of Mexico that the war for Southern independence had ended."

"Hell, you haven't told everybody. Not all your soldiers."

"That is correct. Only those who must know the truth have been told. The rest—the youngest recruits, usually—are best left in ignorance of this lamentable fact." He leaned suddenly closer to Longarm. "And we have most assuredly not told our growing work force of Negro slaves." He smiled coldly at Longarm. "I am sure you can understand why. After all, these darkies are and will continue to remain the primary source of our wealth."

Longarm shook his head in some puzzlement. "Seems to me you'd have one hell of a time keeping a secret like that from them."

"It is difficult, yes. But we manage."

"And you want me to join this...command of yours?"

"Either that, Montana, or die. It would be a simple matter for me to convene a court-martial. A firing squad would end the unpleasantness first thing in the morning. Believe me when I say it would be a welcome diversion for many. Another Union spy caught and punished. It would do much to recharge our flagging patriotism." His eyes regarding Longarm closely, he said, "Well, Mr. Montana, what is it to be?"

"Hell, Colonel. I'll join up. No need to beat me over the head. This may be the perfect place for me, anyway. Like I mentioned before, there's a silly lawman on my tail."

The colonel smiled. "Fine. I am pleased you will be joining my command. However, before we accept you as a recruit, we must wait a suitable period of time. Certain inquiries must be made. I am sure you understand."

"Sure, Colonel," said Longarm, getting to his feet. "Seems like a sensible enough precaution."

The colonel stood up also. "In the meantime, you will be free to make use of our little town. I blush to admit that my soldiers insisted on naming it after me. It has a thriving saloon, and contained therein you will find all the usual vices: drink, gambling, and women. You'll need quarters, fresh clothes, and money, of course. We will be willing to advance you as much as you need of the latter. Unless you are a *very* poor poker player, it should last until our investigation is complete. Under no circumstances, however, are you to associate with or have anything to do with any of our Negro slaves. Is that clear, Mr. Montana?"

Longarm nodded. "Perfectly."

"And I would suggest you not make it your business to inform every young recruit you meet that the War is over. We have seen to it that they would not believe this fact easily. On the other hand, if you insisted on broadcasting this news, we would, I am afraid, find it prudent to silence you. Permanently. You can understand our position, I am sure."

"I won't breathe a word, Colonel."

"Fine. I am looking forward to the time when you will take your place in our officer corps, Mr. Montana. I believe you have leadership qualities. By the way, during the War, with whom did you ride?"

"I rode West, Colonel, with myself in command. Like you, I saw the way it was going."

The colonel nodded, satisfied, and slapped Longarm heartily on the shoulder. "We'll get along, I'm sure."

The colonel walked with Longarm to the door of his study, opened it, and told a waiting orderly to see to Lieutenant Will Montana's needs. Not long after, a pocket in his Confederate uniform heavy with freshly minted gold coins, Longarm strode into Sutpen's only saloon, where he found a table in a corner and was immediately approached by a fiery Mexican bar girl, anxious to get him a drink.

She was Juanita López de Santa Rosa.

Chapter 5

"My, you look so handsome in your new uniform," Juanita whispered as she placed Longarm's drink in front of him.

Hugging him impulsively, she sat down beside him and momentarily rested her head against his shoulder. Then she kissed him lightly on the cheek and sat back, a wicked smile on her face as she savored his astonishment.

Longarm glanced quickly around. There were not too many people in the saloon at this hour, but its cool dimness cloaked them nicely, and Juanita's affectionate embrace was perfectly in keeping with her duties.

"My name's Will Montana now," Longarm told her, "and if I were you, I'd keep out of sight. This here

Colonel Sutpen has an eye for a pretty Mexican lady. Now, how in hell did you get here?"

"I see the oilskin package floating in the water. The one you keep our provisions in. It was caught in the rocks near the shore. I go in the water to pull it ashore when those men come back with you. I stay deep in the water when they look for me in the rocks. Then I follow you and the others over the mountain to this place."

"And they let you in here? Just like that?"

"These girls who work here, they are Mexican like me. They have come with the soldiers when they return from Matamoros. This place, they do not like—but they must stay. When I tell them what happen, they hide me. And now I work for this one who run the place. Now you tell Juanita why you wear this new uniform."

Longarm grinned. "I've just been recruited by a madman. Seems Colonel Sutpen is looking for better men to stock his garrison. But there's a joker in the deck. He's going to investigate me, he says, before he offers me a commission."

"How long you have?"

"Not long, I'm thinking."

"Good. You come with me tonight. I go to see my father and brother. I find where they are. Maybe you come too. There is much trouble here, I am told."

"Trouble?"

"Many slaves hide in hills and there are others who hate the colonel. They want to raise beef, not grow cotton. Some who come here as prisoners have break free and they are very angry. The colonel, he use his soldiers to seek out and kill these people. Maybe you help them. Yes?"

"Maybe I can, maybe I can't. I might want to give

82

it a try, though. How do I meet these people?"

"Tonight I take you to them."

Longarm finished the tequila and stood up. "I'll be here," he said. "Meanwhile, I suggest you take good care of your customers—their drinks, that is."

She grinned and got to her feet. "Yes, Will Montana. Juanita will do that."

A moment later, he stood outside the saloon, squinting in the midday sun as he looked the town of Sutpen over. It was a flimsy, pathetic fake, an attempt to create what could never be again—a quiet, rural Southern town dependent almost solely on the production of cotton, and held together by grand and elaborate courtesies.

The buildings were etched in filigree and whitewashed diligently. Proud horses pulled elegant open carriages through the streets. The women, under their parasols, dressed in the laced-up, suffocating high fashion of twenty years before. The overly attentive men sitting beside them looked like perfumed dandies whose sole occupation was to bow and smirk at the silly creatures. No wonder the colonel was looking for fresh stock. These tender males, products of a sheltered oasis, looked almost as ready to faint as the women. As his gaze took in the entire scene, Longarm was reminded of a time long past—one that he remembered only dimly, and was just as glad he had left behind.

He started back to the barracks that had been assigned to him, intent on getting some more sleep. He was going to be busy this night, and he wanted to be ready.

Longarm was awakened roughly. He opened his eyes and shook off the hand that had grabbed his shoulder. The room was dark and as he sat up, he found Lieutenant

Dumas Tyler standing in the gloom by his bed. Two soldiers with rifles were standing at the foot of his bunk.

"The colonel wants to see you, Mr. Long," said Tyler coldly. "We caught a friend of yours not too long ago—a Mr. Cecil Benton. He has told us a most interesting story."

Longarm swung his legs off the bunk and scratched his head. The jig, it seemed, was up. He could forget his Will Montana masquerade—forget, too, going off with Juanita to meet her friends later this night. Longarm got to his feet and slipped into his shirt, then pulled on his Confederate britches.

"Let's go," said Tyler, nudging Longarm in the back with his pistol. "The colonel is waiting."

The colonel was indeed waiting, as was Cecil Benton.

Benton had been sitting in the chair beside the colonel's desk. On Longarm's entrance, he stood up, his mean, lidded eyes regarding Longarm with malicious triumph. Longarm expected the young man to lick his chops any minute.

"That's him!" cried Benton eagerly. "Deputy U.S. Marshal Custis Long. Like I said, a real nosy son of a bitch."

Longarm was not under physical restraint when he was pushed into the colonel's study. Stepping forward swiftly, he swung on Benton, catching him across the cheek with his open palm. The force of the blow snapped Benton's head around and he had to reach out for the corner of the colonel's desk to steady himself. Two soldiers behind Longarm immediately grabbed him from behind and pulled him back, pinning his arms by his side.

"Let me have him!" squealed Benton in a rage, his right hand held up to his stinging cheek.

"Enough of this!" barked the colonel, glaring with evident distaste at Cecil Benton. "Mind your manners, sir, or I'll have to deal with you first. That loose tongue of yours demands such punishment."

Immediately cowed, Benton slunk back away from the desk, looking uncertainly about him. He had evidently thought to put himself in solid with the colonel by unmasking Longarm. But things were not going as he had planned.

The door opened and a stunningly attractive woman entered. She had gleaming black hair, high cheekbones, eyes like those of a tigress, and a swelling, voluptuous figure that was barely covered by the long green dress she wore. The dress itself was a shameless incitement, starting as it did well off her golden shoulders and not beginning to cover much at all until a generous amount of cleavage had been displayed.

She was of mixed blood, Mexican and perhaps Negro, Longarm realized. But it did not matter, really; the result was so spectacular. He watched her move silently across the heavily carpeted floor to the colonel, who had risen at her entrance and moved out from behind his desk to greet her.

"Bascom," she said, her voice soft and enticing, "it is late. You promised to read to me again tonight. I have been waiting."

"Violet," the colonel said, his voice suddenly muted, almost gentle. "I have important business that must be transacted. I will be with you as soon as I can. Go back and wait for me. I won't be long."

For a moment Longarm thought Violet was going to pout and protest her dismissal, but then she leaned her exquisite face against the colonel's and whispered something to him. Delighted, the colonel blushed. Laughing softly, mischievously, Violet drew back from the colonel, turned to gaze boldly about her at the men in the room, then strode from the study. When the door closed behind her, Longarm felt a collective sigh pass around the room.

But Longarm could not shake the feeling that something about the scene he had just witnessed was not what it appeared to be on the surface. Something in the girl's eyes, and the manner in which she had entered and left the room, troubled him vaguely.

Clearing his throat, the colonel looked coldly at Longarm. "You do not deny you are a United States marshal, Long?"

"No sense in that now, I reckon."

"And why is the Yankee government curious about me? What do they know, Marshal? I might still find a place for you in my ranks if you'll cooperate."

"I'd sooner bunk in a hog wallow than join your ranks, Colonel."

"Quite right." The colonel looked at Tyler. "Take Long out and shoot him. And don't waste any time about it."

"Shouldn't we wait until morning, Colonel?"

"Why?"

"There'll be more light for the firing squad."

"Use torches. Besides, enough bullets will find a home, I am sure. It doesn't have to be neat, just so it gets done."

"Yes, sir."

86

"And take this mealymouth with you," the colonel added, glancing distastefully at Cecil Benton.

As one of the orderlies reached out for him, Benton backed up in horror, his eyes wide in disbelief. "But, Colonel!" he bleated. "You can't do this. I cooperated. I pointed out a spy in your midst."

The colonel turned and looked at Benton the way one would at a noxious vermin scurrying out from under a rock. "If there's one thing I can't stand, Benton, it's a turncoat. You are the son of a United States senator. Yet you turned in an agent working for your own government. I am doing your father a service."

Sobbing in terror, Benton was thrust out of the room ahead of Longarm, and soon the two of them were marching through the moonless night toward the army compound.

Longarm was lying on his back in his bunk in the same cell where he had spent the previous night. His head resting back on crossed arms, he stared up at the ceiling, grateful for the cooling breeze coming in through the barred window beside him.

In the next cell a distraught Cecil Benton was pacing miserably. The lieutenant had gone off to muster a firing squad. Longarm was thinking of Juanita, waiting for him in the saloon. He hoped she would be able to get her father and brother out of this madman's world, but he was not too hopeful.

The tramp of footsteps broke the silence outside the guardhouse. A sharp, unfamiliar voice could be heard issuing orders to the firing squad, warning its members to shoot carefully, no doubt. Longarm heard something closer by, just outside his window. A footstep. He swung off his bunk, went to the window, and peered out at the moonlit yard.

Juanita's face appeared in the window. "Here," she said, thrusting a lariat and an ancient Colt through the bars at him.

He thrust the Colt into his belt and knotted the lariat around the window's bars. Juanita disappeared from sight. In the next cell, Benton was watching, his mouth agape. Longarm tossed the Colt through the bars at him.

"Here," Longarm told him. "Shoot your way out, if you've got the stomach for it."

As Benton scrambled for the gun, Longarm heard the slap of a quirt outside the window. A quick explosion of hoofs followed. The rope grew taut and with a sharp, grating sound, the bars were ripped out of the window, taking portions of the adobe sill with them.

At that moment, the guardhouse door swung open and a corporal strode in, with two members of the firing squad at his back. Longarm did not wait. He dove for the window, arms and head first, squirmed through, and dropped to the ground. Scrambling to his feet, he saw Juanita riding toward him, leading a saddled horse. Ducking swiftly aside, he snatched the reins Juanita handed him and swung onto the second horse.

As he galloped off with her, he heard shooting followed by cries of anger and surprise coming from the guardhouse. A moment later the soldiers broke out of the guardhouse and began firing at them, the rattle of their rifle fire filling the night.

Keeping his head low, Longarm called out, "Where are we heading?"

"Look for a farmhouse with a road going past it. Then we cut for the hills."

Longarm was pleased that Juanita knew where they were going. The only trouble was, how far could they go—really? They were trapped in this infernal valley with a pink-cheeked but reasonably efficient Confederate army close on their heels.

Chapter 6

When they reached the farmhouse Juanita had mentioned, they were met by a small contingent of the Confederate troops, with Lieutenant Dumas Tyler in command. Longarm pulled up in astonishment as Tyler and his men crowded around him. Tyler saluted Juanita and nodded in greeting to Longarm.

"I see she got you out of there all right, Long," he said.

"She did, Lieutenant. Was that your idea?"

"It was, but she insisted on taking care of it herself."

Juanita explained to Longarm. "I knew it be much more easy for me to ride through to the guardhouse because the young soldiers, they are very eager to help me. I tell them my horse go lame, so they lend me new horse." She laughed and pointed at the horse Longarm was riding. "But it get well fast, Longarm. *Si?*"

"Si," Longarm replied.

He looked back at Tyler. "It looks to me like you're on our side now. Do you care to explain that?"

"Later, Long. We've got some riding to do."

"All right. Later, then."

With a wave of his arm, Tyler set the escort off, heading in the direction of the hills that lay directly north. A small covered wagon was with Tyler's contingent, and Longarm assumed it was crammed with munitions and other supplies. A good idea. If they were going to fight the colonel, they would need supplies and plenty of ammunition to begin with. That was for damn sure.

They rode through the night at a steady pace and Longarm's amazement at the breadth of this hidden valley grew with each hour that passed. Soon they were in hilly, wooded country that appeared reasonably well watered. The longer they rode, the more often he sighted cattle.

At dawn they pulled up on the crest of a broad tableland that gave an almost uninterrupted view of the valley Colonel Sutpen called his own. As he and Juanita dismounted, Tyler approached them.

"You might say this is the beginning of our stronghold," Tyler told them. "At least this is where we have decided to make our stand."

"You mean you're going to fight him?"

"You forget I have been privy to his plans. He has been readying his men for this offensive against the dissidents up here for some time. He calls them traitors, and he is determined to wipe them out, once and for all."

"And you think this small band of yours can stand against that madman?"

"It will not be so small a band when the time comes, Long. Colonel Bascom Sutpen is at the end of his tenure. The fact that Washington has sent you to investigate makes that abundantly clear to everyone. You'd be surprised to learn how fast the news of your capture spread through the valley. We take it as a sign that Sutpen's insane charade is about to come crashing down upon his head."

Longarm shook his head in exasperation. "Why in hell don't all of you just get out of this here canyon? Abandon Sutpen to his darkies and his cotton. Just get out."

"No. This canyon is ours just as much as it is his. Our children have grown up here. Our families are here, our friends. We have created fertile farmland where once it was close to desert, where only the mesquite prospered. Up here in these hills is excellent graze. We are not going to abandon what we have built up for the last sixteen years to that licentious, evil old man."

Looking past Lieutenant Tyler, Longarm saw a familiar and striking figure being helped from the covered wagon by Tyler's men. At first he did not believe his eyes.

It was Violet. The covered wagon had held not munitions but Colonel Sutpen's mistress.

Excusing himself, Tyler left them and hurried over to Violet. The moment she saw him, Violet flung her arms about his neck. Longarm could hear her sobs of joy clearly from where he was standing. The woman was obviously close to a nervous collapse, and seemed quite groggy. Tyler caught her up in his arms and carried her over to a tent his men had already set up for him.

"How do you like that?" Longarm asked Juanita, shaking his head in wonderment.

"I do not know if I should like it or not, Longarm. Is there something wrong? That is Tyler's woman, is it not?"

"That's what it looks like, all right. But the last time I saw her she was Sutpen's mistress—or wife, I'm not sure which. At any rate, I reckon the lieutenant's right. The colonel will be up here shortly. He's got an added incentive now. Maybe we'd better get some shut-eye."

Juanita smiled. *"Bueno.* I have your things with me. I take them from the river. Do you remember? And I have your bedroll, too. You remember how it keep us warm?"

Longarm grinned. "I remember."

They led their horses into a stand of cottonwoods, and not until they had finally bedded down did Longarm realize how exhausted he was. Juanita was tired, too. Pleased though they were to be sharing the same soogan, there was no urgency left in either of them for anything other than sleep.

The blazing noon sun and the sound of the camp stirring below the trees awoke them. Not long after, fully dressed and well fed from the makeshift mess Tyler's quartermaster had set up, Longarm and Juanita walked through the bustling camp, astonished at the number of soldiers they saw. Just as the lieutenant had predicted, many more of the colonel's disgruntled men had joined Tyler's command since the night before.

Longarm looked around for Tyler and saw him standing beside the covered wagon. The lawman started toward him. As he and Juanita approached the lieutenant,

Violet emerged from the wagon and climbed down beside Tyler.

She was dressed in a simple dark blue dress, a much less flamboyant outfit than the one she had worn in Colonel Sutpen's mansion. Nevertheless, she was still a spectacularly beautiful woman. Now, however, Longarm noted, there was no longer that vague, unfocused look about her. She seemed vibrantly alive to the world about her and most notably to Lieutenant Tyler's presence.

As she took her place beside Tyler, she nodded almost shyly to Longarm and Juanita.

Tyler had seen Longarm's close scrutiny of Violet. "Marshal Long, that woman you saw last night in Sutpen's house was not in full command of her senses," he explained, taking Violet's hand. "Sutpen has been filling Violet with hellish drugs. Opium, and God knows what else. He's a devil, that one. This poor girl is only the latest in a long line of innocent souls that monster has despoiled. She's just one more reason why we are going to take this land from him." He smiled and indicated the crowded camp with a motion of his hand. "You see? As I told you last night, our forces have grown considerably."

"I noticed, Tyler. But even so, I wouldn't count that madman out too quickly."

A rifle shot sounded from the lookout on a ridge high above the camp. A moment later a sentry came running.

"It's the colonel!" he cried. "He's got the whole division with him!"

Longarm turned to the lieutenant. "Looks like you'll be starting that battle sooner than you expected, old son."

Tyler nodded grimly and helped Violet back up into the wagon. Longarm and Juanita hurried into the cottonwood grove and mounted up. A moment later, he and Juanita headed for the hills Juanita had been told about earlier. As they galloped off, they heard the sound of small arms fire erupting behind them, and then—much later—the ominous thunder of cannon.

Colonel Sutpen was anxious to get his mistress back, it seemed.

As Longarm rode steadily north through the hills, he could not help noticing the broad aqueduct or canal that wound beneath them, slicing a neat, brilliant swath along the canyon floor. There was no doubt that the colonel had wrought a marvel. Madman though he was, he had managed to transform a bleak canyon into productive land.

By nightfall they had left the hills and were riding across a moonlit landscape, dodging around the chaparral as best they could, when the sudden beat of hoofs surrounded them. Pulling up swiftly, they found horsemen closing in on all sides. The cold gleam of gun barrels showed clearly in the moonlight.

"All right, you two," someone called. "Who are you and what're you doing here?"

It was Juanita who spoke up. "I seek my father, Juan Lopez de Santa Rosa. He is with the family of Billings."

"Hey, Billings!" someone called.

The call was repeated and, a moment later, a horseman pushed through to them. "I'm Lyman Billings, ma'am," he said. "And who might you be?"

"Juanita Lopez de Santa Rosa," she replied. "Is my father with you?"

The man's bluff, square face brightened instantly.

"Why, sure he is, ma'am. And you'd be his daughter! Now, how did you manage that? Getting in here, I mean?"

"This man with me, Deputy U. S. Marshal Long. It was his doing."

Billings glanced quickly at Longarm and stuck out his right hand. "Aha!" he cried, shaking Longarm's hand warmly. "You're the one we been hearin' about! News travels fast. Have you come to help us throw that old tyrant into jail?"

"I was sent to check on a wild story—that hidden away in one of these canyons a Confederate colonel had an army of his own and was waiting for the Confederacy to rise again."

His face sober, Billings nodded grimly. "It wasn't such a wild story, after all, was it?"

"No, it wasn't," Longarm agreed.

The rider who had spoken first holstered his gun and nudged his mount closer to theirs. "The colonel has already begun his offensive, Heywood. We'd better get back to your place. We got some plannin' to do."

The reunion of Juanita with her father and younger brother was touching, and it was with tears in her eyes that Juanita introduced Longarm to them. Their eyes, too, were filled with tears of joy as they grasped Longarm's hand in gratitude.

Longarm could see that Juanita was giving him too much credit, and was trying to convince them that she was exaggerating when a sweat-soaked rider burst into the adobe house.

"I just heard," he cried, "the colonel's got past Tyler

and his renegades. And he's still coming. Looks like this time the crazy son of a bitch is bound and determined to wipe us out."

From a ridge a mile below the Billings ranch, Longarm and Billings, with his party of thirty or more ranchers, watched at noon the next day as the colonel, astride his white horse, sent his troops ahead of him over the hilly terrain toward Billings's waiting forces. The colonel's youthful army, resplendent in fresh uniforms and gleaming buckles, marched in perfect formation, their rifles resting on their shoulders, the steady beat of their drummers growing louder with each passing second. Soon Longarm could hear the fife's high, shrill piping as well.

Earlier that day Billings had been joined by the remnants of Tyler's force, with Tyler himself—slightly wounded and utterly exhausted—riding into the ranch with Violet soon after. Though Tyler and his men had insisted on joining Billings's force when they rode out to meet the colonel, Longarm and the others would not allow it, for they were too spent and discouraged to be of much help now.

Peering through the heat waves billowing up from the baked ground, Longarm could see no cavalry or artillery. From Tyler's account of his own defeat, Longarm and the others knew that the colonel had both cavalry and a punishing artillery and would employ them as soon as Billings and his small band made a stand. For now, the colonel was keeping them well back, somewhere out on the flanks, Longarm was sure.

Longarm had already convinced Billings and his men not to make a stand on this ridge. Instead, they would let the colonel's infantry march on through unopposed, while Billings split his small mounted force and sent them after the colonel's artillery and cavalry. If they found either, they might possibly manage to mount surprise flanking attacks that might succeed in neutralizing them both, after which they would be in a better position to overtake and deal with the colonel's fuzzy-cheeked infantry.

The regular, monotonous beat of the drums grew steadily louder. The fife's shrill cries pierced the sunlit air, reminding Longarm dimly of another battle many years before. The memory of it came unbidden and caused a slight shudder to pass over his powerful frame. Around Longarm, the riders who were going with him fidgeted anxiously, waiting for his signal.

Longarm could see the sun glinting off the infantry's individual rifle barrels by this time. He could not see the colonel, however. Abruptly, the foremost ranks of soldiers appeared on the crest of a gully less than two hundred yards distant.

"Now!" Longarm cried, spurring his mount to the right, his riders following him almost as one body.

They galloped hard, leaving the neat ranks of marching men well to their left, and crested a ridge. Nothing. Galloping down into the draw, Longarm decided to stay in the depression. The going was slow, since the draw was littered with boulders, but they kept on, and were amply rewarded about a mile farther on when they came out on the flanks of the colonel's artillery struggling up a steep incline.

Taken completely by surprise, the colonel's men abandoned their field pieces to meet Longarm's charge. The fight was swift and deadly. Firing a Winchester from his hip, Longarm accounted for two soldiers, one of whom he peeled back off a caisson. The force and the suddenness of the charge demoralized the soldiers and after a short, bloody battle, they flung their weapons down and surrendered.

Dismounting to tally the dead and wounded, Longarm counted only two wounded men on his side, while the artillery had lost four dead and two wounded. Longarm was sorry to see how young the dead artillerymen were. He cursed the colonel bitterly as he turned away from their vacant faces. Detailing five men to round up the caissons and return with them to the Billings ranch with the wounded from both sides, Longarm sent the healthy prisoners on a march back the way they had come, without boots and weaponless. Then he saw to the burial detail.

After a short respite, Longarm and his men mounted up and continued on, following a vast flanking movement designed to encircle the colonel's forces. They had traveled no more than a couple of miles when they heard gunfire ahead and spurred their horses toward the sound. Rounding a low mesa, Longarm saw Billings and his men engaged in a ragged, uneven battle with the colonel's cavalry. Colonel Sutpen's men appeared to be winning, since they outnumbered Billings's riders two to one. There was no need for Longarm to give his men any orders. They snatched their Winchesters from their scabbards and spurred their mounts into battle.

With their reins wound around their saddlehorns and their Winchesters belching lead in rapid fire, Longarm's men cut through the pink-cheeked cavalrymen. The surprise of Longarm's forces completely demoralized the colonel's men. The battle was short and vicious. Horses and men went down as clouds of dust billowed up about them, obscuring the battlefield and the combatants.

When the dust cleared and the firing came to a halt, less than half of the colonel's cavalrymen were still in their saddles, and those who were had lost all stomach for further battle. Swinging their horses about, they galloped off, heading back the way they had come.

This time, however, the casualties suffered by Billings's men were not insignificant. As Longarm moved about the battlefield, he could not help noticing once again how youthful were the faces of the colonel's dead.

It was plain to see what had been happening. Once the older members of Sutpen's narrow little kingdom became aware of what a monstrous fraud the colonel was perpetrating on his subjects, he had lost their allegiance. As a result, only the youngest of the colonel's soldiers could be trusted by him to bear arms to perpetuate his mad rule.

It was well into the afternoon when Longarm's and Billings's combined forces returned to deal with the colonel's infantry. Encountering no resistance to their march, they were now deep into the hills, less than a mile from Billings's ranch. There was no sign of the colonel, Longarm noted as he spurred his weary mount on.

The moment Longarm and his men were spotted by the colonel's infantry, they dispersed swiftly, taking cover behind bushes, boulders, and what few cottonwood trees dotted the dry hills. Dismounting, Longarm and the others took up positions themselves and proceeded to return the somewhat spiritless Confederate fire. The young soldiers, it appeared, had marched for long hours without issue, and were obviously weary and dispirited.

Still, their fire was accurate, and Longarm could see a few platoons gathering themselves together under the verbal lash of their officers. Soon, he had no doubt, they would attack.

As Longarm crouched down behind a boulder and levered a fresh cartridge into his firing chamber, he searched the enemy position for some sign of the colonel. If they could just manage to take that man, this madness would be over in an instant.

"You seen the colonel?" Longarm asked one of his men as the fellow joined him behind the boulder.

"Sure! Behind you!"

Longarm turned about. High atop a ridge the colonel, dressed in full Confederate regalia and still astride his magnificent charger, was beckoning with a gleaming saber at his troops below. He was signaling them to fall back—to retreat.

The colonel must have just learned what happened to his artillery and cavalry, Longarm realized.

At once the fire from the infantry dropped off, and a moment later Longarm watched as the colonel's remaining force pulled out.

"We've won!" cried Billings, hurrying over to join Longarm, a triumphant grin on his face.

"Not yet, we haven't," said Longarm. "He'll be back."

"I reckon that's the truth of it, Long. But now at least we got ourselves a breather. And this here's the first time Colonel Sutpen's had to retreat. He knows it now. From here on out, he's in for a battle royal."

Longarm nodded and stood up slowly. He was extremely tired. But it was not just this day's battles and the hard riding that made him so weary.

It was trying to accept as indisputable fact that the bizarre events of this afternoon actually had taken place—that he really had just finished skirmishing with elements of a Confederate army in Texas, fifteen years after Lee surrendered to Grant.

Chapter 7

The time had come for stock-taking. It was a week later, and the ranchers had gathered in Billings's ranch house with Longarm and Tyler to discuss their next move. Crowded into the large kitchen, most of them had managed to secure a place around the huge deal table. Longarm sat at its head with Tyler beside him. No longer as certain as he had once been that Colonel Sutpon could be stopped, Tyler was letting Longarm do most of the talking.

At the moment, however, Longarm was simply listening as the ranchers went over once again the dismal conditions under which they were trying to operate their holdings. With depressing rapidity, the colonel had rallied his demoralized forces and sent his cavalry back in to roam the ranchers' tableland and hill country at will. They swept through the land, burning and pillaging with all the ferocity and bloodthirsty effectiveness of Quantrill's Raiders, a tactic urged on them no doubt by the colonel himself.

Worse even than the loss of the ranchers' buildings was the loss of their beef cattle and horseflesh, most of which the colonel's cavalry had already driven off. And, though many of the valley's inhabitants who chafed under Sutpen's rule were heartened by Longarm's presence and the promise of revolt he brought with him, many others— the townspeople of Sutpen especially—were now thoroughly aroused by this rebellion. They were quite well aware of what privileges they would lose were the insurgents to succeed in deposing the colonel, and were filling his ranks with fresh and eager recruits.

Now, as the ranchers and the few remaining renegades from the colonel's forces discussed their situation, many expressed the fear that if the colonel were to send his army into the hills after them a second time, it would meet precious little opposition.

"Oh, we'll stop him," Tyler protested doggedly. "We stopped him once. We can stop him again."

A strained silence greeted this assertion, and a few looked away from the lieutenant, unwilling to meet his frank gaze. Longarm looked up to thank Juanita for the coffee she was placing in front of him, then cleared his throat. All eyes turned hopefully to him.

"Let me ask you all once more," Longarm said, unable to keep the weary exasperation out of his voice. "Why don't you simply leave this valley with me? Later you can return with the U. S. Cavalry. Those men will make short work of Sutpen's forces."

"Getting out of here is not that easy," explained Ed Munger, a rancher who lived close to the canyon rim. "I've tried many times to build a trail that would enable me and my stock to reach the canyon rim, but the walls are too steep. There's a single, narrow game trail. But you'd have to be a goat to use it safely—and a lucky one at that."

"And that river is no help," broke in Simon Waller. "You should know that, Long. It almost killed you and your lady friend. And many's the slave that's tried to go that way. The rapids took them all, I'm told."

"Besides," said Billings wearily, "once we abandoned this place to bring in Union forces, who's to say we would ever be able to lay claim to our land again. We'd lose everything. No, we've got to stay here and fight or we will have nothing for all these years of labor."

"All right," Longarm said wearily. "Then I have a plan. See what you think."

"Go ahead," said Simon Waller. He leaned forward to listen, his bald pate gleaming in the lamplight. "I'm about ready to try anything at this point."

"All right, then. What about the slaves? Has anyone let them know yet that they are now—by the laws of these United States—free and independent citizens who can neither be bought nor sold?"

A hush went around the table. In that instant, Longarm realized suddenly why the slaves still toiled from dawn to dusk without a murmur, even though they were surrounded by whites who had known for years that the Civil War was over. The reason was quite simple. For all of them—Southerners born and bred—the thought of a free Negro was a kind of blasphemy. They had been able to accept the Confederacy's defeat, but to accept

107

also the fact that the Negroes whom they were accustomed to buying and selling were now free men—equal to themselves in all things—was more than they could handle.

Longarm leaned back in his chair and watched them. He could see in their faces confusion, even outrage, at his words. But he also saw their struggle to accept what he said and go on from there.

"All right," said Ed Munger, stroking his yellowing walrus mustache shrewdly. "So now all them darkies're free men. What about it?"

"I suggest we tell them," Longarm said. "I suggest we point out the implications of their new station as well. If we succeed in this, perhaps they might even be able to give the colonel enough aggravation to divert his attention from us."

"You mean start a slave revolt!" cried Coop Hamner, a red-faced fellow with large, pale blue eyes. He had been sitting at the end of the table, but was now on his feet, his eyes wide with anger. "Do you know what you're suggestin', Marshal? I'll have none of it!"

"Not a slave revolt, but something just as effective," Longarm explained patiently. "What would happen if they simply stopped working, and demanded payment for their services? Wouldn't that bring the colonel's economy to a sudden halt?"

Ed Munger stroked his mustache and chuckled softly. He turned to look at Coop Hamner. "Sit down, Coop, and keep your shirt on. The marshal's got a point there. If we want to stop the colonel, what better way?"

The rest joined with Munger in approving the idea. Coop Hamner sat down slowly, then reached for the cup of raw whiskey in front of him. Longarm relaxed, then leaned forward to explain his scheme.

Two days later, a little after midnight, Longarm and Lieutenant Tyler left the cottonwoods lining the irrigation canal, ducked across a narrow road, and disappeared into a sprawling shanty town that housed most of the slaves who worked in and about the town of Sutpen.

With Tyler leading the way through a confusing maze of alleys and narrow streets, Longarm found himself at last crossing a littered back yard. Ducking under a clothesline, Tyler pulled up before a door and knocked. There was no answer. He knocked again, louder. From within someone told whoever was knocking to keep his britches on.

Tyler stepped back, relieved. The door swung open and a huge Negro stood in the doorway, a lantern glowing in his right hand. He looked in some irritation at Longarm, then held the lantern close to Tyler's face.

"Why, Lieutenant Tyler, suh," he said, his voice deep. "What you doin' in Sam Bigger's back yard this time a nights? The colonel chase you this way, did he?"

"Never mind that, Sam. Can we come in?"

Bigger stepped back, holding the lantern out so his visitors could see their way into his place. As Sam closed the door behind them, Tyler told him it might be a good idea to put out the lantern. He did not want to get Sam in trouble. Bigger blew out the lantern and placed it down on the floor by the door.

Longarm blinked quickly to adjust his eyes to the sudden darkness as Bigger and Tyler sat down at the kitchen table. While Longarm pulled up a rickety chair,

Tyler introduced him to the black man. Sitting down at the table, Longarm stuck out his hand. For a moment Sam Bigger hesitated to take Longarm's offered hand. Then, with a wide grin, he shook it warmly. Slaves, Longarm realized, were not used to shaking white folks' hands.

Longarm spoke up. "Sam, Tyler here tells me you don't take kindly to working from dawn to dusk—among other things. He says you've been occasionally chastised by the colonel for your independence, as he calls it. That right?"

Sam Bigger nodded. "That's the way of it, Mr. Long. I been a hard darky to satisfy since they sold my woman on me ten years ago. I don't much care now what the white folks do to me. They already done the worst."

The man's deep voice rumbled softly as he spoke, but Longarm had felt the abiding pain in the man's words. Choosing his words carefully, he said, "Sam, the War Between the States is over, and has been for close on to fifteen years now. The Union won and the Confederacy has been disbanded."

Sam Bigger's massive shoulders lifted as he turned his head to look in some surprise at Tyler. "I heard some tell of this, Lieutenant Tyler," he said, his voice hushed in surprise. "But I never had reason to believe it. This here's the first white man to tell me it's the truth. Is it?"

"It's the truth, Bigger," said Tyler.

Sam Bigger looked back at Longarm, his dark, liquid eyes glowing in the moonlit room. "Why you come here in the middle of the night to tell this here nigger the War's over, suh? What you up to?"

"I'll come to that later," Longarm told him. "There's something else I want to tell you first."

"I'm listenin'."

"Abraham Lincoln signed a proclamation before the War was over, freeing the slaves. You are a free man, Sam Bigger. As free and independent as I am and Lieutenant Tyler is. No one owns you or any of your family or any of your friends." Longarm leaned back in his chair to study Sam Bigger's reaction. The big man was just sitting there staring at him. "Did you hear what I just said, Sam?"

Bigger nodded incredulously. Then, eyes wide, he got slowly to his feet. Turning to look at Tyler, he said, "Now see here, Lieutenant Tyler, suh, what's this all about? How come this friend of yours comes to Sam Bigger's place in the middle of the night to tell me such a outlandish story?"

"It's no story, Sam," Tyler replied. "It's the truth. Every bit of it. You're a free man, no matter what the colonel tells you or wants you to believe."

"It's that simple, Sam," reiterated Longarm. "You're a slave no longer. And, legally, you've been a free man for more than fifteen years. The colonel just didn't want to tell you."

Sam Bigger looked down at his powerful hands, then placed his palms against his chest as if he were trying to ascertain his true measure as a free man. A wondering smile grew on his face. "Me?" he said. "Sam Bigger a free man? You mean I ain't a slave no more?"

"That's the long and the short of it, Sam," said Tyler. "Get used to the idea."

Laughing softly, Sam leaned his head back. "Sam Bigger's free!" he exulted. "It's the God's truth! I been hearin' things, and now I aim to believe what I been hearin'!"

111

"You got anything to drink in here?" asked Tyler.

Sam nodded eagerly. "I got some corn whiskey, suh."

"I think you owe us and yourself a drink to celebrate. Don't you, Sam?"

"Why, sure, suh. Yassuh! Right over here under the sink."

Swiftly, his hands shaking slightly in his eagerness, Sam Bigger produced a jug and three pewter mugs. He poured generously, and a moment later the three men lifted their mugs and drank to Sam Bigger's birth as a free man.

Afterwards, there was a momentary, almost hushed, silence. Longarm broke it. "What are you going to do now, Sam?"

"I don't know, suh. I just got to get used to the idea, that's all. But I figger it'll take a while for me to do that."

"And after you get used to the idea?"

He smiled then, his white teeth gleaming in his dark countenance. "I aim to go see that colonel and ask him why he been keeping my people in chains all this time. He shouldn't oughta done that. No, suh."

"What makes you think he'll tell you?" Tyler asked.

Sam Bigger frowned. He poured himself another mugful of the whiskey and downed it as casually as if it were a glass of water. "Guess maybe he won't tell me, nohow. Never knew that man to give a nigger the time of day. Guess he'll just go on laughin' and swingin' that whip of his."

"So what are you going to do?" persisted Longarm.

"I told you," Sam growled, "I don't know. I don't know."

"Who's your master, Sam?"

"Mr. Beauregard Whitman, suh."

"He owns the general store in town," Tyler told Long-arm. "Sam's his teamster."

"Are you going to work for Mr. Whitman tomorrow, Sam?" Longarm asked.

Sam Bigger frowned. "No," he said with sudden decision. "I ain't."

"You going to tell him—or anyone else—why you won't be working?"

Sam Bigger thought that over for a moment. Then he reached for the jug once again and poured his third drink. "Yassuh. I'm going to tell him. And I'm going to tell all my friends, too. I don't think none of us niggers should work tomorrow. No, suh, I don't!" He gulped down his third mugful of whiskey, then glared balefully across the table at Longarm.

Longarm got to his feet. "I think you ought to spread the truth, Sam," he said quietly. "Start tonight. Why wait? Why should any of you go to work tomorrow, for the colonel or anyone else? No one can force you to work any more. Not even the colonel. You are all free men."

Tyler stood up and Longarm glanced at him. "Let's go, Lieutenant. We've got a long way to go."

Longarm and Tyler walked to the door. Sam Bigger hastened to open it for them, then stepped back to let them out. A moment later, as Sam Bigger stood in the open doorway and watched them go, they hurried off through the night.

"Well," said Longarm wearily, "we tossed the match onto the tinder. Now we'll just have to wait to see if it catches fire."

Tyler shook his head. "I don't mind telling you, I'm discouraged. It doesn't look to me like Sam Bigger is going to do much more than get drunk on cheap rotgut."

"Hell," said Longarm, wiping his mouth with the back of his hand, "Bigger's whiskey wasn't all that bad."

They were almost into the cottonwoods along the canal when a dark shape stepped out of the trees ahead of them. The vaguely familiar figure held a shotgun leveled at Longarm and Tyler.

"Hold it right there," Cecil Benton snarled.

"Godawmighty," Longarm drawled in sudden exasperation as he recognized Benton's voice. "What the hell are you doing here, Benton?" he demanded.

"Thought I was dead, didn't you?" Benton crowed. "You threw that gun to me so I'd get cut down while you got sprung. Ain't that right?"

"I wanted to give you a fighting chance. Now I'm very sorry I did that, Benton, believe me."

Benton chuckled meanly. "I believe you. Drop your weapons, both of you."

Longarm and Tyler unbuckled their gunbelts and let them fall to the ground. Juanita had retrieved and returned to Longarm his .44 and what she called his whore's gun. The derringer now rested in the back of his right boot.

"Now step over there. Pronto!" Benton said, waggling the shotgun to his right.

As soon as Longarm and Tyler had moved, Benton snatched up the fallen weapons, then told the two men to start walking ahead of him down the narrow, rutted road.

"What the hell are you up to, Benton?" Longarm demanded angrily.

"I been hiding in this damned shanty town," Benton snarled, "with the only thing between me and the dirt floor a complaining nigger woman. You can imagine

114

how pleased I was earlier when I saw you and this crazy Confederate slip through my back yard."

"You talk too much, Benton," barked Tyler. "Where are you taking us?"

"To the colonel. He don't much like me, but maybe he'll change his tune some when I haul you two in. I been hearing a lot about this here revolt so I figure I'm going to get a big, fat reward for bringing you two in."

"Don't bet on it, Benton," said Tyler.

"You keep moving. I'll do the betting."

It wasn't long before Longarm saw the colonel's mansion rearing out of the moonlit gloom ahead of him. Shrugging wearily, he kept moving. He should have been worried, he realized, but he wasn't.

By this time, Cecil Benton was more of a comic relief than a menace.

Chapter 8

Once Benton reached the colonel's front porch, he held up and emptied his shotgun into the air. Lanterns were lit inside the mansion and a captain hurried from the house with a huge revolver in his hand. He pulled up in some confusion when he saw Longarm and Tyler standing on the gravel path under Benton's guard.

"What in blazes is goin' on here, mister?" the captain demanded of Benton. "Did you just fire that shotgun?"

"I did. Tell Colonel Sutpen I have captured Lieutenant Tyler and Deputy U. S. Marshal Long."

The fellow hesitated, then turned and went into the mansion. A moment later he reappeared and directed Benton to bring his two captors inside. Keeping a sharp eye on all three of them, he showed them into the colonel's study.

The colonel, awakened by Benton's shotgun blast, had dressed hurriedly and appeared more than a little annoyed. His silken white hair was in some disarray and he was dressed in a long wine-colored robe.

"Stay, Captain Smythe," he told the officer as he eyed Benton and his two captives. "I may need your assistance."

"Colonel," Benton announced proudly, "I captured these two in the shanty town. I know how anxious you are to have them."

"You do, do you?"

"Of course. These are the leaders of the rebels you have been fighting in the hills."

"And you expect to be suitably rewarded for this, I expect."

Benton took a deep breath and nodded confidently. "You were hasty before, Colonel. You didn't treat me right. I can be of great help to you in this business. My father is—"

"Enough from you!" the colonel snapped, peering at Benton as if he were some kind of vermin. "You are a turncoat, I say. A traitor!"

"But, Colonel," Benton resumed desperately, "I just want to show you that I hold no grudge." Longarm saw beads of sweat standing out on Benton's forehead.

"Smythe!" roared the colonel. "Take Benton's shotgun from him!"

Benton offered no resistance as the captain took the weapon. Turning back to the colonel, his face as pale as a bedsheet now, Benton flicked out his tongue to moisten his dry lips. It was an unsettling, almost obscene gesture. Never before had Longarm seen a man this terrified.

"Take this turncoat downstairs," Colonel Sutpen told Smythe. "Put him in the same cell with his prisoners." He smiled bleakly. "We'll see how young Mr. Benton likes that."

"No!" Benton cried. "I won't go. I came here to help you, Colonel. I brought these men in. I captured them."

Ignoring Benton, the colonel fixed his gaze on Tyler. "You took Violet," he said to the lieutenant, almost sadly. "How is she?"

"As soon as she rids herself of the drugs you fed her, she'll be fine."

The colonel sighed. "Don't be so sure of that, Lieutenant." He looked at Tyler with some affection. "She has stolen your good sense, as she did mine, I'm afraid. I suppose you think you love her."

"I do love her," Tyler maintained stoutly.

"And of course she loves you."

"Yes."

The colonel laughed, coldly, pityingly. "I should free you. The truth of that woman—that Jezebel—will cause you more pain than I could ever manage to fashion. But I will not free you. You have bitten the hand that fed you, Lieutenant, and brought others to death and ruin as you importuned them to follow your benighted course."

"Do your worst, Colonel. I only regret that I did not turn my back on you sooner."

"Take him and that sniveling turncoat out of here, Smythe," the colonel snapped.

Smythe opened the study door and waggled his revolver. Terrified, Benton slunk toward the door, Tyler on his heels. As Longarm was about to follow them, the colonel called out to him, "Hold it there, Long. I'd like a word with you."

Longarm turned to face the colonel. Smythe continued out of the room with Benton and Tyler, pulling the study door shut behind him.

"I asked you once before to join my forces, Long," the colonel said, getting to his feet and moving out from behind his desk. "I'm asking you again, but for the last time. I suggest you think it over carefully before you give your answer. Those fool rebels no longer need you or Tyler. They are done for. Their stock is gone, their ranches destroyed. They'll be coming in soon, a ragtag band of fools, anxious to make peace." He shrugged. "And who knows? I can be merciful. They are like children. All they really needed was chastisement."

"I don't have to think it over, Colonel. You are a madman. A tyrant. I wouldn't join you under any circumstances. And I wouldn't cook my chickens before they were plucked, if I were you. This rebellion isn't over yet."

The colonel's pale face darkened. "Mad, am I?" he thundered. "Look about you! See what I have created in the middle of this cursed land! I have turned the desert into a garden, have created wealth where before there was only desolation."

"Sure, Colonel," Longarm drawled. "I see what you've created here. A place where you can strut around like God Almighty, creating wealth out of the toil of slaves who should long since have been freed."

"Have it your way, then," the colonel snapped, his voice harsh. Taking a small revolver from his bathrobe pocket, he held it on Longarm. "Come with me. I'll lock the cell door on you myself, Marshal."

Without warning, a large rock crashed through one of the French windows. It bounced across the desk and narrowly missed the colonel before it struck the wall. Another rock followed the first, completely demolishing another of the French windows. Glancing out the window, Longarm saw torches glowing in the night and for the first time heard the surging roar of an angry crowd sweeping closer.

Sam Bigger, it seemed, had begun to spread the good news.

"Here comes the source of your wealth, Colonel," said Longarm. "Looks like they know something they didn't know before. They are no longer slaves, but free men. And it sure as hell is making them angry, looks like."

The colonel rushed to the window. "Damn you, Long! This is your doing."

"Reckon that's right, Colonel."

The colonel spun to face Longarm, raising his revolver. Longarm throught of the derringer in his boot and realized he would not have time to reach for it. But before the colonel could pull the trigger, another rock came crashing through a side window, followed this time by a flaming torch.

Instantly, the window drapes caught fire. Distracted, the colonel looked in the direction of the flaming drapery. Longarm did not hesitate. He rushed the man, knocked him flat, and kept going toward the French windows. Head down, he lowered his shoulder and plunged through. Emerging in a shower of broken glass and window sash on the patio outside, he found himself facing a crowd of angry, torch-bearing slaves who were rushing up onto the lawn, heading for the mansion.

They had no way of knowing who he was. As far as any of them could tell he was one of the colonel's men.

As some of them surged toward the mansion, others came for Longarm, their crude clubs upraised. Longarm tried to outrun them, but they swiftly overtook him. Blows began to rain on his head and shoulders. Then someone caught him about the thighs and flung him to the ground. Rolling desperately in an effort to present less of a target, Longarm saw a giant of a black man part the ranks of those bent over him as he flung Longarm's assailants aside with astounding ease.

It was Sam Bigger. He reached down and hauled Longarm to his feet. "You better get away from here, suh," he said. "These here slaves have done gone crazy."

Longarm thanked him and hurried off. Slipping carefully through the darkness to avoid being sighted by other roving gangs of outraged slaves, he headed for the town. When he reached it, he found it filled with roving gangs of slaves who took particular delight in knocking out store windows and shouting out for all the world to hear that they were free—free at last.

He was ducking into an alley to escape one such rock-throwing mob when he heard a familiar voice calling down to him from above.

"Hey! You down there!"

He glanced up to see a red-headed woman leaning over the railing of her window balcony. It was the madam Tyler had called Samantha, the one who had asked Tyler if her girls could have first crack at Longarm.

"Go 'round the back!" she called. "I'll be down to let you in."

He found the back door and waited in its shadows as four or five torch-bearing slaves rushed through the alley past him. When they were gone, the door opened a crack and he slipped inside. Taking his sleeve, Samantha led

122

him up the narrow, winding back stairs to her room.

"Phew!" she cried, closing the door behind her. "What a ruckus! You mind telling me what this is all about?"

"Not at all," Longarm told her, slumping into an easy chair to get his breath. "The slaves have just learned that they are no longer slaves—that some seventeen years ago, Lincoln signed the Emancipation Proclamation."

"That so?" Samantha said, moving out onto her balcony and looking down at the running figures. "I guess it's about time them poor devils found out. It's a wonder they didn't get wind of it before this."

"Samantha, how about a drink?"

"I could use one myself."

She poured them each a whiskey. He took his straight, she added water to hers. Then they went out onto the balcony. The colonel's mansion was burning briskly in the distance, as were one or two places of business further up the street. The citizens of Sutpen were swarming out into the night now to fight the fires and drive back the celebrating slaves. Bucket brigades were formed in front of the burning buildings while other men, armed with rifles and handguns, took after the roving bands of blacks. The sound of gunfire crackled in the night.

Longarm knew it was over for the slaves when the Confederate cavalry galloped into town and proceeded to charge into the alleys and narrow streets, firing without compunction into their midst. Even when the colonel's men had succeeded in dispersing the slaves, they would not let the matter rest there. Individual cavalrymen hounded the slaves mercilessly as they fled into the night. The despairing cries of the wounded and dying floated up to them on the balcony, filling the night air with horror.

The brief, pathetic rebellion petered out as the first rays of dawn peeked over the rim of the canyon. The colonel's mansion was no longer burning, but a few burnt-out buildings in Sutpen were still smoldering, and everywhere Longarm and Samantha looked, they could see bodies lying in the dark, bloodstained dust. Some of the dead were white, but the majority were black. Without firepower, all the slaves had been able to do was set a few fires, grapple with a few white men—and get themselves killed.

"You'd better stay here for the day," Samantha said, pulling Longarm from the balcony. "You can't leave here until nightfall, I'm thinking."

Longarm was too weary and too dispirited to argue. The colonel was still alive and well, he was sure. The revolt, though it had altered much, had not really accomplished what Longarm and Tyler had hoped.

Colonel Sutpen's tyranny was still intact, and there seemed no way now for them either to leave this place or to bring him down. And soon the colonel would march on the rebels who still remained in the hills and wipe them out, just as he had boasted.

And there would be no one to stop him.

All he and Tyler had really succeeded in doing was to muck things up for the slaves. Free or not, they would be forced to continue to work for their ancient masters, the only difference being that now, at least, they would know that freedom waited for them outside the confines of this narrow valley. In that respect, this was the dawn of a new day for Sutpen's mean little kingdom.

Samantha undressed Longarm and slid him into her bed, covered him, and kissed him lightly on the forehead.

He looked through a fog of weariness up at her and managed a smile. Then he slept.

When he awoke, it was late in the afternoon, and Longarm was aware of an enormous hunger. It felt as if a small, angry animal was burrowing through his vitals. He sat up and looked around the room. It was empty. Throwing back the silken sheets, he swung his naked body around and stood up.

Samantha entered, fully dressed, holding a loaded tray in her hand. Her eyebrows shot up when she saw Longarm standing by the bed. After appraising him coolly for an instant, she turned and closed the door firmly behind her.

"I could smell that food all the way up here," Longarm told her unabashedly as he sat back down on the bed and pulled a sheet up over his lanky nakedness. "I think that's what woke me."

"I hope there's enough here for you," Samantha told him. "The cook is wondering why I wanted so much steak and potatoes—not my usual diet at this time of day." She placed the tray down on a night stand beside the bed and flipped the gleaming white napkin back, revealing a thick steak smothered with onions, fried potatoes, and four thick slabs of homemade bread spread lavishly with melting butter. The coffee was almost intoxicating in its aroma.

Longarm ate with a gusto that delighted Samantha. When he had finished, he glanced up at the madam with real gratitude. "Best meal I've had in a long time, Samantha. My compliments to the cook."

"I wish you'd go down and talk to her," Samantha

said ruefully as she took the tray and placed it on a marble-topped table by the door. "She wants to quit now that she knows the slaves have been freed."

"Why not pay her?"

"I don't dare. Colonel Sutpen has already issued a proclamation of his own. Anyone who pays a slave for working will be shot. And he would do it, too. There's no doubt in anyone's mind about that."

"No doubt in my mind, either," said Longarm ruefully. "He survived intact, I gather."

"He was wounded slightly, I understand. But nothing serious. And he was able to save most of his house. They are already at work on it, repairing the damage." She sat down beside him on the bed. "I suppose it's a good thing the slaves have found out what all of us have known for years," she mused thoughtfully. "There's no need to be so fearful now that they will find out. They have found out, and what difference has it made? Like the rest of us, they are still trapped here."

"How did you come to this place, Samantha?"

"The colonel recruited me. Just as he has recruited every Mexican or Indian girl in this house and the saloon next door. First, of course, he tastes the delicacies himself. Then, when he tires of his plaything and craves some new delight, he sends his men out for more recruits."

"You say he sends his men out. And I know he trades with Matamoros. If he can freight cotton and other goods out and ship back such 'delicacies' as you mention, why in blazes is it so impossible to get out of this place?"

"You remember that steep road you followed when you were escorted in that night? The one blasted out of the rock face?"

"I remember it."

"It's guarded night and day by the colonel's most trusted men. And think of how exposed that trail is. Anyone who tries to make it up to the ridge that way—and many have tried, Longarm—is easily spotted. No one has made it all the way to the top. And if they do, there's a welcoming committee waiting for them. Then, if they survive all that, there's the river."

"All right. But how do the colonel's teamsters get their freight wagons across the river and into Mexico?"

"Five miles south, the canyon walls on each side of the river are close enough for a drawbridge to be lowered across it." She smiled. "The colonel was an engineer before the War. The pieces for the drawbridge are carried in the freight wagons and quickly bolted together on the spot. It's very clever, Longarm, you must admit."

Longarm sighed in frustration. "Yes, I suppose it is. The son of a bitch seems to have thought of everything." Longarm looked at Samantha. "But there *was* one slave who did manage to escape this valley not too long ago."

Samantha frowned in concentration, then nodded quickly. "Oh, yes. You mean old Ben. I remember. He was the colonel's manservant." She shook her head as she recalled the incident. "They brought him back and buried him in the colonel's private graveyard in back of his place. Everyone was shocked that the colonel would bury him there alongside the bones of decent white folks."

"Before they killed him," Longarm told her, "he contacted a captain in the cavalry. That's why I am here."

"You should have brought the cavalry with you, Longarm. I think you're going to need it."

Longarm sighed as he nodded in agreement. He

glanced out the window. The last rays of the setting sun were striking the tops of the curtains, turning them a rich orange. The sound of activity in the street below seemed perfectly normal. Business as usual in Sutpen.

He looked back at Samantha.

She returned his gaze, then leaned forward impulsively and kissed him boldly, hungrily, on the lips. He took her in his arms and pulled her onto the bed beside him.

Without a word, she pushed herself upright and slipped out of her dress. While her fingers worked, she smiled at him and spoke softly. "I ain't worked in the cribs for a long time, Longarm, and to tell you the truth, it's been a week now since I've had a man. I saw what you have when I came in, so don't be gentle with me. I want all of it—every inch."

Then she was naked before him. There was nothing skinny or malnourished about her. Her ample breasts rode high on her ribs, and her legs and thighs were powerful and milkwhite. She saw his appreciative gaze and leaned back on the bed so that he could take all of her in at his leisure.

"If you see anything you like," she said, "just help yourself."

He moved up onto her, straddled her, then leaned forward and kissed her on the lips.

"You ain't supposed to kiss a whore on the lips," she whispered.

"You maybe saved my life last night. Right now, a whore you are not." As he said this, he leaned down and kissed her again, then let his lips nibble at her earlobes for a spell. He felt her stirring voluptuously under him. She reached up and flung her arms about him.

He dropped his lips onto her erect nipples and flicked each of them with his tongue, rapidly. She moaned and reached for his shaft. "You don't have to pleasure me no more, Longarm. Just go on in. The door's wide open, waiting for you!"

He let her guide him into her and was surprised at how tight she was. Groaning with delight, she declared he was almost too big for her and began to move her hips. He could feel the warmth of her swallowing him. It had been a long time for Longarm, too. Remembering that she had told him not to be gentle, he let himself go.

A moment later, in a wild fever of thrusting and flailing at each other—resembling combatants as much as lovers—they came, then sagged, exhausted, into each other's arms.

"Oh, my God," she murmured as she clung to him. "It's been so damn long since I had someone like you! So damn long!"

He chuckled and nibbled on her earlobe again. "Now, that makes me feel right proud, it does."

"You should be proud. You know how to pleasure a woman. You surely do."

He chuckled and moved his lips down her chin and began kissing her neck. He heard her soft moan. "Again, Longarm," she whispered.

"You sure?"

"I am insatiable, Longarm."

He kissed her belly, then moved back to her breasts, crouching over her again, his erection pulsing eagerly once more. He closed his mouth around her breast. She moaned, then sank her teeth into his shoulder, biting almost hard enough to draw blood. He leaned quickly over and took her other breast in his mouth, roughly.

129

Groaning, she spread herself to receive him, her legs raised high, her educated hips rolling and rising under him as he plunged once more into her. Again he found her as tight as a clenched fist.

"Slowly," she whispered huskily, her head flung back, both arms about his neck. "That's it! Oh, so nice and slow. Yes . . . !"

Each time he felt her nearing her climax, he slowed to a stop, plunging fully into her hot depths, holding her tightly and pressing in as deeply as he could go without motion. Each time her breathing eased and her cries died away until he began thrusting again.

But he could manage such control for only so long. Soon, he was stepping up his tempo, aware that he was in a headlong flight to his own climax—and hers. He soared above her, bringing her with him to a final, dazed explosion that left them limp and motionless.

They said nothing as their panting subsided. He rested his head upon one of her breasts, and she put her arms around him and held him against her body. The warmth of her lulled him. He felt his senses spinning away into delicious tides of sleep.

And then he became aware of her hands moving expertly over his limbs, exploring every secret part of him. She had shifted so that he was on his back under her, while she leaned her face over his, the moist tip of her tongue tracing his eyelids and ears, then trailing mischievously down his belly and even further. Her hands had already brought him nearly erect once more, and now, as her tongue darted wantonly, his erection peaked.

In that instant she was astride him, plunging down upon his shaft. He heard her gasp, then whimper as she came, shuddering. But, for her, this was only the beginning. Longarm clapped his big hands over her hip bones and plunged her down onto him. She uttered tiny little cries as she arched herself back over his quivering flanks. He began to thrust violently upward. As his momentum increased, she hung on, delighted, her lips parting in a smile of pure delight. Groans began to break from deep within her throat. She was riding him now with eyes squeezed shut, her hair a scarlet cloud about her head. Releasing her hips, Longarm reached for her breasts and hung on to them as she rocked with demented abandon above him.

"I'm coming!" she cried. "I can't wait!"

"Then don't!" he told her, laughing up at her.

With a piercing cry, she swept into her orgasm, her juices flowing freely now, running onto his belly and down his thighs as his callused hands held onto her breasts. Though he had been intent only on pleasing her, he now felt himself, miraculously, building once again, moving swiftly beyond the point of control. With a cry, he soared up into her as his own violent spasm wrenched him violently. At last he was spending himself deep within her, exploding, gushing furiously.

With a happy sigh, Samantha sank down upon his chest and enclosed him in her arms and hugged him close, as if she were attempting to will his erection to remain forever within her. But he realized, achingly, that there was no way she could do that now.

He was strong and reasonably healthy, but as he had found once before when pleasuring a woman who had come to him—he was not immortal.

Chapter 9

The cook's name was Hattie. Samantha had convinced
the woman to come up to her apartment on the second
floor to discuss the excitement of the night before, and
now she sat on the red velvet sofa so cautiously that
Longarm was afraid she was going to fall off at any
moment. The luxury of Samantha's apartment intimi-
dated her fearfully, even though she had served Samantha
and her girls in this house for years.

Hattie was very thin with long, nervous fingers she
held clasped in her bony lap. She was wearing a faded
white, featureless sack of a dress, and had a red polka-
dot kerchief tied about her head.

Throughout Longarm's gentle questioning of her,
Hattie's big, liquid eyes regarded him with a mingling

of fear and respect, while her responses to his questions revealed a considerable body of information concerning the abortive uprising of the night before.

"... and you say Sam Bigger is being held in the colonel's mansion?" Longarm asked. "You're sure that's where they're keeping him?"

She nodded quickly. "They's taken him to them dungeons, yas, suh. And them's terrible places. That colonel, he's a devil. He does frightful things to them he takes down there. Poor Sam. He caught it for sure this time."

"When did they capture him?"

"This afternoon. He was hidin' in them trees near the canal when they found him."

"And you say others have been imprisoned as well?"

"Yas, suh."

"Hattie, are any of your people still willing to fight back?"

Her eyes widened in surprise at the question. "Oh, yas, suh! They sure is! My people, we don' like bein' slaves!"

"Fine! Now then, by any chance did any of them manage to get hold of any weapons last night?"

Straightening up for the first time and leaning her back against the sofa, she said, "Yas, suh. They sure did get some guns."

"Where are they hiding?"

Hattie swallowed, then glanced uncertainly at Samantha.

"Go ahead," urged Samantha. "Tell Mr. Long, Hattie. Maybe he can help Sam Bigger and the others."

"In shanty town," Hattie said, looking back at Longarm. "In a place the white folks never go near—the

dump. We got ourselves real fine hidin' places in there."
She looked almost proudly at Longarm. "The rats, they's
our guard dogs."

Samantha shuddered. But Longarm was pleased. Now
all he had to do was get to those men. Perhaps, with
their help and their weapons, he could manage to pluck
Tyler and Sam Bigger from the colonel's grasp—and
maybe even bring down the colonel himself.

"Hattie, I need someone to take me to those men.
Tonight. There's no time to waste."

She nodded. "I know someone. Jed Taylor. He has
a horse and wagon. He picks up the white folks' trash.
I'll get him to stop out back tonight and tell him where
you want to go."

Longarm got to his feet. "That's fine, Hattie. I ap-
preciate it."

She got to her feet also and looked up at Longarm.
"If'n you get Sam Bigger free, you tell him Hattie helped.
You do that?"

"I sure will, Hattie."

She smiled then. "I noticed him. But he never noticed
me. Seems a shame for a big man like that to live all
alone just because the colonel sold his woman down the
river."

"I'll tell him that," Longarm promised.

Samantha showed Hattie out, closed the door, then
turned to him, her arms out. He stepped into them and
hugged her for a moment. Then he stepped back and
looked down into her emerald eyes.

"How long do you think it will take for Hattie to
contact that junk collector?"

"Not long."

"Do we have enough time to say goodbye?"

"Just enough," she said, taking his hand and leading him into the bedroom. "But not nearly as much as I want."

As soon as Jed Taylor slowed up, Longarm darted from the doorway and climbed into the rear of his wagon. He found himself burrowing into junk of all sizes and description. Sharp edges abounded, along with the sad smell of burned things. He found the blanket Hattie had told him would be there for his use, pulled it about him, and coiled up in a corner of the wagon, just behind the driver. The old Negro driving the wagon had not looked back or said a word when Longarm flung himself aboard. He said nothing now as he turned his wagon onto the main drag.

For a while all Longarm could see was the tops of some buildings, then nothing as he heard the sharp clop of the nag's hoofs as they proceeded over the wooden bridge. Soon they were following the road that ran alongside the canal. Poking his head up cautiously, Longarm saw the dim, confused outline of shanty town less than a mile ahead of them.

They were almost there, and Longarm was beginning to congratulate himself on getting out of Sutpen so easily, when he heard the sharp gallop of a hard-riding horse coming at them from the rear. He ducked his head back down swiftly.

In a moment the rider had overtaken the wagon and was galloping along beside them. "Pull that wagon over, nigger!" the rider shouted. "What in blazes you doin' out here this time of night?"

The seat beneath the old man creaked as he yanked back on the reins and brought his nag to a halt. "I's jest takin' junk away is all, mastah," he protested. "After all that burnin' and killin' las' night there's a heap a things the white folks want taken away. And I found lots of things I can use. So I'm headin' for the dump now."

"At this time of night?"

"I been real busy, mastah. All day. They sure was damage done, and a lot of things got broke."

"I don't trust you, nigger. I ain't never goin' to trust another one of you again. Get down off that box. I think maybe I'd better have a look through this junk you say you're bringin' to the dump. The colonel says some of you niggers have firearms hidden away."

Longarm heard the squeak of the cavalryman's saddle as he dismounted, then the tread of his boots as he walked alongside Jed Taylor to the rear of the wagon.

"Now see here," Jed protested. "You ain't gon' take my junk, is you? I been collectin' it all day!"

A thump and the sound of a slight scuffle told Longarm that the cavalryman was not being at all gentle as he flung the old man to one side.

"Damn your black hide!" the cavalryman spat. "You get out of my way and stay out. Just stand over there while I check this here junk of yours."

The wagon shifted as the cavalryman stepped up onto its bed. Longarm heard the man draw his saber from its scabbard and then the sound the blade made as he thrust it about at random into the mattress and chairs and other pieces of junk. The snick of the blade sounded closer with each passing second, and Longarm knew he was going to have to make his move fast.

He would have drawn the derringer from his boot, but he did not want to fire a shot for fear the sound of it would only bring more cavalrymen. Waiting until he judged the cavalryman was close enough, Longarm threw his blanket aside and flung himself up at the dark figure.

Longarm was lucky. The cavalryman's saber was extended, its blade caught in the cantle of a worn-out saddle. Before he could retrieve it to strike at Longarm, the big lawman caught him about the neck and drove him violently backward. Clawing frantically at Longarm's tightening fingers, he stumbled off the wagon. He hit the ground first, landing heavily on his back. Longarm remained on top of him, his fingers continuing to close, vise-like, about the cavalryman's windpipe.

Thrashing wildly, desperately, the cavalryman clawed Longarm cruelly about the face and neck. But Longarm ignored it all as his fingers continued to dig into the soldier's neck. His tongue thickened in his mouth and his eyes bulged grotesquely out of their sockets. Desperate to finish it, Longarm tightened his fingers about the man's windpipe with a sudden, wrenching thrust and felt the bones give way. The crunching snap they made cut through the sound of Longarm's labored breathing. At once the cavalryman lay still beneath him.

Panting deeply, aware of a painful constriction in his chest, Longarm released his fingers, pushed himself off the dead man, and got shakily to his feet. Flexing his fingers painfully, he turned wearily to Jed Taylor. The old man had been watching the struggle with wide, terrified eyes. When Longarm turned to him, he took an involuntary step backward.

"I'm going to get into this man's uniform," he told Jed. "I'll be riding alongside the wagon all the way to the junkyard. If anyone stops us, let me do the talking. Right now I want you to help me strip the body and then throw it into the wagon under this junk."

Moistening his lips, the old man nodded obediently, and soon they had peeled the uniform off the cavalryman. Longarm let the unhappy old man push the stiffening corpse in under the junk, while he climbed into the dead man's uniform.

There were four slaves hiding in the junkyard, all of them desperate to escape, since each of them had been spotted by their white masters the night before. The Negroes' weapon cache amounted to four Winchesters, two Henry repeaters, a double-barreled shotgun, and four Colts. The only rounds they had were those still in the firing chambers. The cavalryman Longarm had killed had provided him with a gunbelt filled with cartridges, a Winchester, and a Colt.

Not much to start a war with, Longarm reckoned, but perhaps it would be enough. Leaving Jed Taylor behind, Longarm selected one of the four Negroes to drive the wagon in his place. Then, with Longarm riding alongside as an escort, they set out through the night for the colonel's house.

They had almost reached it when a single horseman rode out of a cottonwood stand and ordered them to halt. Reining his mount in, Longarm kept the wagon between him and the cavalryman as he explained that he was bringing in some uppity slaves he thought might know something about those missing arms. He was taking them to the colonel for interrogation.

"Good idea," the rider said, moving away into the night. "The colonel will know what to do with them, sure enough."

When they reached the colonel's mansion Longarm directed the driver to pull up in front of it and wait.

Dismounting, Longarm pulled his cavalryman's wide-brimmed hat well down over his face, mounted the porch steps, and crossed the porch to the front door. Before he reached it, the captain Longarm had met earlier opened it and stepped out.

Longarm's saber sliced past the man's ribs and through his heart. With barely a sound, the captain slipped to the floor of the porch. Longarm beckoned to the waiting Negroes, who poured swiftly and silently out of the wagon and followed him into the mansion.

Lanterns were glowing dimly all about. Everywhere Longarm looked, he saw fresh scaffolding, evidence of the rebuilding and repairing going on as a result of the fire. The smell of burnt wood and furniture hung heavy in the air. Though Longarm did not know how to reach the colonel's dungeons, one of the biggest of the slaves did. His name was Ned. He had once been a guest of the colonel in those same dungeons.

Ned led them down a steep, spiral stairway cut out of the earth and lined with sandstone slabs. Niches carved out of the wall above the stairs held small oil lamps. They guttered fitfully but gave off enough light to enable Longarm and the others to see the way.

At last Ned pushed through a door and they found themselves in a long corridor lit by smoking brands planted in iron brackets on the walls. Two guards, dressed only in Confederate britches and slippers, were sitting at a table, slumped forward on their crossed arms, two empty bottles on the table before them.

They looked up blearily as Longarm's party approached, but did not have the time to cry out as they were clubbed into insensibility.

Individual cells led off the corridor. Huddled in them were terrified Negroes and a few Confederate soldiers who had joined Tyler's brigade on the tableland. As Longarm and his men peered in at them, they stirred sluggishly, unable to believe their good fortune. Longarm detailed two of his men to release the prisoners and arm those who were well enough to use weapons.

None of the cells contained Tyler or Sam Bigger.

Longarm continued along the corridor until he came to a large door. Ned appeared to hesitate momentarily as he pushed past Longarm and pulled it open for him. Entering, Longarm found himself in a large, high-ceilinged room, lit like the corridor with smoldering torches attached to the walls.

In the torches' flickering, garish light, Longarm saw Sam Bigger, Cecil Benton, and Lieutenant Tyler hanging from hooks in the center of the room. Beneath their raw, naked bodies, charcoal fires glowed.

"Get them down!" Longarm cried hoarsely as he hurried in.

Kicking the braziers out from under the three men, he sent the glowing coals flying, then looked up at them. The hooks holding them were attached to chains depending from the ceiling.

By that time, Ned and two other men were beside him. Longarm reached up and began the messy, grisly task. The hooks had been skillfully placed so that no vital organs or muscles were ruptured, since the colonel was concerned that his playthings not die prematurely. Nevertheless, when the men were lifted off the hooks, their wounds were reopened, and soon the three naked bodies were streaked with fresh-flowing blood. The char-

141

coal fire had done its job as well. The legs and lower torsos of all three men had been seared raw, their skin peeling off in strips.

When at last their tormented bodies came to rest on the dungeon floor, all three of them came awake to shriek out their agony and had to be knocked unconscious in order to be carried from the place.

Halfway up the narrow stairway, Longarm heard the door above them open and the pounding of boots as two or possibly three guards rushed down the stairs toward them. They had probably just discovered the dead captain on the front porch, Longarm realized.

He vaulted up the stairs to meet them, a saber in his right hand, a Colt in his left. On his heels came Ned with the shotgun. The first guard plunged down the stair-well and pulled up less than three feet from Longarm, whose Confederate uniform momentarily confused him.

That delay was fatal. Longarm thrust home his saber, impaling the man just below the belt. As the fellow sagged forward, his companion, rushing down the stairs behind him, slammed into his slumping form. Before he could bring up his Colt, Longarm struck him unconscious with a single downward sweep of his gun barrel. A shouted query from above told them that more guards were on the stairs. Bursting past Longarm, Ned charged up the stairwell. Longarm heard two shattering blasts from Ned's shotgun, and when he reached the top of the stairs he had to pick his way over two bloody corpses.

Ned was waiting in the corridor, his empty shotgun on the floor behind him. Longarm handed him his saber. The big fellow took it with a grin and cut the air with it twice to get accustomed to its heft.

Behind Longarm, the released prisoners poured out

of the stairwell. Longarm led them from the mansion and watched carefully as Tyler, Bigger, and Benton—all still unconscious—were placed down as gently as possible in the back of the wagon. Longarm sent a man into the mansion for clean blankets, which were wrapped carefully around them.

Few of the released prisoners, it turned out, dared or wanted to return to shanty town, since they knew that if they did, they would be hunted down and killed on the spot. When Longarm asked them what they wanted to do, those able to travel said they would like to flee into the hills with Longarm, Ned, and the others. Tyler's cavalrymen were equally anxious to go with Longarm.

"We'll need horses," Longarm said. He turned to Ned. "Are there any in the stables out back?"

Ned nodded. "Many horses, suh. And fine, pretty wagons, too."

"We just need horses. The only men we'll take with us are those who can ride."

Ned nodded.

Longarm looked around. The night seemed peaceful, almost preternaturally still. The crickets in the shrubs and grass about them were making an unholy racket. The gunfire inside the mansion had evidently been muffled enough that it had not brought any of the colonel's men running. And because of the fire's extensive damage, the grounds were practically deserted, with the colonel and his household staff undoubtedly sleeping elsewhere.

Glancing toward the town, he saw no lights. Satisfied that they were in no immediate danger, Longarm told Ned, "All right. Take the wagon and those coming with us to the stables. Saddle them up and wait for me."

"Where you goin', suh?"

"I want to finish off this mansion for good."

Ned smiled. He knew what Longarm had in mind.

"I'll need about fifteen minutes," he told Ned. "Be ready."

Leaving Ned in charge, Longarm hurried back into the mansion. Picking up lanterns as he moved, he proceeded from room to room, pouring oil over the floors and walls. He made sure to visit the dungeon as well, and was on his way out of it when he noticed a door leading from the large torture chamber where they had found the three men.

Opening the door, he saw that it led onto a narrow passageway. Peering into it, he saw a short flight of steps at the far end. Longarm frowned. He had discovered a hidden annex, he realized. Holding up the lantern he had been emptying to give him light, he took out his Colt and proceeded down the passageway to the stairs. Mounting them softly, he came to a narrow landing, pushed open another door, and found himself in a dim anteroom, the only light coming from a crack under a door on the far side of it.

He knew at once what he would find when he opened that door—for the moment he stepped into the anteroom, his senses had been assailed by the sweet, cloying smell of opium.

Putting down the lantern, Longarm moved lightly across the room and rested his ear against the door. As he listened, he opened his mouth slightly to reduce the sound of his breathing and became aware almost at once of the low murmur of voices and the occasional, delighted trill of a woman's laughter that came from the room beyond.

Stepping back, Longarm planted his foot squarely

against the door and pushed. The flimsy lock gave easily as the door swung wide. Stepping into the room, his Colt held out in readiness, Longarm found himself in a spacious bedroom, its walls a riot of colorful drapes, the bed itself enclosed in a spectacular red silk canopy. The air of the room was alive with shifting curtains of blue smoke, through which everything was only dimly perceived—lending a fantastical air to the bedroom and its occupants.

Ghastly white in his nakedness, Colonel Sutpen lay on the bed with two women—one black, the other a shimmering, intoxicating gold. The women were coiled about him like serpents. The colonel laughed when he saw Longarm before him. It was a startlingly high, feminine laugh.

Then he sat up and held out an opium pipe to Longarm.

Without hesitation, Longarm aimed his Colt at the colonel and fired through the shifting coils of smoke. But his senses were reeling by this time, and he was only sure that the gun had detonated because of the way it jumped in his hand. Indeed, its round seemed to have no effect whatsoever on the colonel, who continued to laugh—the sound of it reverberating hollowly in Longarm's ears.

He brought his Colt up to fire again, but heard a woman chuckling beside him, and spun to see Violet advancing on him, a gleaming Turkish scimitar held high over her head. He ducked back just in time as the blade sliced the air inches from his face.

The force of the swing threw Violet off balance. She staggered past him and collapsed to the floor, the scimitar in both her hands. Looking up at him, she began to laugh—a low, throaty murmur that made the hair rise

145

on the back of his neck. Longarm stepped back, unable to believe his senses. The last time he had seen Violet was back at the Billings ranch. She was waving goodbye to Tyler as he rode off with Longarm.

"Get him!" shrieked the colonel. He had lunged to his feet on the bed and was shrieking at Longarm with maniacal fury. "Get him, my pets!"

The two women were standing on each side of the bed. The Negro woman was aiming a shotgun at him, the other a small, gleaming Smith and Wesson. Longarm threw himself to the ground as the shotgun's blast filled the room with its thunder, planting a ragged hole in the wall behind him. Throwing one wild shot at the shrieking colonel, Longarm dove back out through the open door and plunged down the short flight of steps just as the second blast sent a wad of buckshot after him.

As he raced down the passage and out through the far door, he could still dimly hear Colonel Bascom Sutpen's maniacal laughter.

Chapter 10

The large torture chamber went first. Racing out of the annex, Longarm flared a sulfur match to life, dropped it, and fled out the door and down the passageway past the cells. He turned before he reached the stairs leading up into the mansion and saw the black smoke coiling out through the door after him. A series of thunderous *whomps* sounded as more pools of oil caught fire, and suddenly the flames raced out the door and along the corridor toward him.

He turned and bolted up the winding staircase. Dropping sulfur matches as he went, he moved swiftly through the mansion. Halting at the rear door, he turned and looked back to see the flames racing across the floors and flaring hungrily up the walls. He left the building and ran toward the stables.

In a moment, with Longarm in the lead and with Ned and the others mounted protectively around the wagon containing the three unconscious men, the large contingent of Negroes and whites rode swiftly back to the canal road and began their flight from the colonel's stronghold.

Upon reaching the stables earlier, Longarm had found the grounds about them littered with the bodies of clubbed and garroted white men—and one old Negro. As they rode out, Ned explained almost apologetically that they had had no choice but to handle the stable hands and hostlers as they did for fear that they would have raised an alarm, arousing the Confederate encampments stationed just outside the town. The death of the one old slave bothered Ned the most. But the man had seemed determined to stop them, his loyalty to the colonel stronger, it seemed, than any he felt toward his own race.

Looking back now, Longarm saw the darkness behind them flare with garish light as the mansion exploded into flames. Longarm smiled in grim satisfaction. This time the destruction would be complete. Embers shot skyward and the explosive sound of cracking beams came to him like dim gunshots. As the flames transformed the night around the mansion to broad daylight, Longarm saw mounted soldiers milling about, while others tried to rush into the mansion to save what they could.

Longarm was hoping fervently that Sutpen had been caught in that exploding maw of flame and smoke, but he had little confidence that such would be the case. For a brief while back there in the cellar of that mansion, Longarm had almost been willing to believe he had found the earthly domain of the Prince of Darkness himself. This sense was gone now, but not his conviction that in Colonel Sutpen, Longarm had a clearly diabolical opponent whose tenacious troops were certainly sufficient to wipe out the puny bands of dissidents now awaiting Longarm in the hills about Billings's ranch.

This conviction aroused in him a deadening sense of futility. In order to banish it and replace it with some sense of urgency, he swung about in his saddle and shouted to Ned to hurry the formation along. They were dawdling, he told them angrily. Then he turned about and raised his horse to a gallop. They would have no chance at all if they did not reach the foothills before daybreak.

And as he rode, Longarm promised himself he would not—at least for now—remind himself of what they could all expect in the weeks ahead.

A month later, just as Longarm feared, Colonel Sutpen and his youthful Confederate troops made a ruthlessly successful drive against the dissidents and sent them reeling into the deepest, wildest reaches of the vast box canyon.

Billings and a still weak Tyler did their best to prevent the retreat from becoming a rout, but at the end of it, when the exhausted men and woman saw the walls of red rock hemming them in, the sense of despair was so powerful that some of the men counseled turning on their tormentors in one last furious assault. At least then, they argued, they would die with their boots on.

But this feeling was only a momentary gasp of despair, and soon the calm fortitude of the women and the wan, frightened faces of their children calmed the men somewhat and set them to rebuilding.

It was not easy. This was the driest and most infertile region of the canyon. Arid for most of the year, the rain came down in fierce electrical storms, when it did come, sending flash floods sweeping over the landscape, gouging out fresh arroyos, and sweeping everything, even boulders, before it.

On the flats, mesquite chaparral and cactus dominated. The prickly pear cactus grew to a height that in some cases dwarfed a horse and rider, but at least the few remaining stock the ranchers possessed were able to feed on its leaves. Desert willow, cottonwood, and salt cedar crowded out other vegetation near streams and ponds, but were useful for the most part in giving indication, even at some distance, that water was present.

Worse than the flash flooding and the arid landscape were the rattlesnakes, scorpions, and vicious packs of javelinas that abounded, the latter terrifying the women and a constant danger to the children. Resembling small boars, the javelinas had thick gray bristles and were the color of rats. They fed principally on rattlesnakes, mice, and rabbits, but their most spectacular characteristic was their powerful, musky stench. The oversized scorpions bothered the men the most; no man was safe if he didn't shake out his boots before pulling them on. And meanwhile, despite the hordes of ravenous javelinas, the rattlesnakes were everywhere.

But these transplanted Southerners were as tough as old leather. Many of the men had ridden with Colonel Sutpen before he had turned his back on the Confederacy. So now, even though they could not be certain that the colonel would be content simply to drive them into the most inhospitable reaches of his tiny empire, the men set about constructing cottonwood houses and barns. Before long, corrals were flung up and wells dug. Within a month four families had established themselves in the region, with Longarm and Tyler patrolling it with what remained of their troops.

Longarm crested a ridge and when he saw what lay below him, he reined in so swiftly that his big gelding shook his head in annoyance. Folding his arms, Longarm shook his head in amazement.

"What's wrong?" asked Tyler, reining in alongside the lawman.

Ned and Sam Bigger rode up on the other side of Longarm and halted also. Behind them, the other four members of their troop halted as well, their mounts practically disappearing in the dust their sudden halt raised.

Longarm pointed. "That dam! And the reservoir!"

Tyler laughed. "What about it?"

"Where in tarnation did it come from? You mean it's been out here all this time?"

"Of course," said Tyler. "Hell, that's the first thing the colonel built when he settled this canyon."

"The colonel built it?"

"Sure. He's an engineer—or was, before he joined the Confederate Army."

Longarm nodded. Samantha had already told him that. As he let his eye scan the impressive expanse of water impounded by the crude but powerful dam, he found himself remembering also the roadway the colonel had blasted out of the rock and the collapsible drawbridge he had created to enable his wagons to cross the Rio Grande.

"So this is what feeds that irrigation canal," Longarm mused aloud. "This is the source of the canyon's fertility." Longarm glanced at Tyler and shook his head.

151

"I thought that canal came from a diverted stream. I had no idea the colonel had created anything so massive as this."

"Oh, it's massive, all right," Tyler said. "I was a boy when the dam was built, and you should hear the tales I heard concerning its construction."

"What tales?"

"Quite a few workmen lost their lives. The colonel drove them all without mercy. But when the dam was completed and the canal filled up and began distributing the water to the irrigation ditches, people forgot what a hell it had been to build it."

"I guess they would, at that," Longarm agreed.

He looked carefully now at the massive breastworks, constructed of cottonwood logs and earth, that held back those tons of water. Considering the materials the colonel had had at his disposal, it was an engineering marvel. Despite himself, Longarm was impressed.

It was almost too bad Longarm was going to have to use the colonel's skill against him.

"What's feeding the reservoir?" Longarm asked.

Tyler pointed to a canyon slicing into it on the other side. Longarm had to shade his eyes in order to see it and the stream it contained.

"It's a tributary of the Pecos, I think," Tyler explained. "And there are other, smaller streams emptying into the reservoir as well. Whenever we have one of our cloudbursts, the flooding off those cliffs adds considerable volume to the lake."

Longarm nodded. The dam spanned the narrowest portion of a secondary canyon that extended for some miles before it shunted sharply and ran into the main canyon. Impounded behind the dam was a reserve of water that extended for almost a mile back before it lapped against sheer cliffs. The height of the dam, and therefore the volume of water it impounded, was impressive. At its highest point, the walls of the dam stood as tall as a three-story building.

"I'd like to take a closer look," Longarm said.

"This as as close as you're liable to get," Tyler said. "The colonel's troops guard this dam night and day. Look there. And there."

Longarm looked in the direction Tyler was pointing and realized that what he had thought were just abandoned construction buildings were in reality barracks—two of them, one at each end of the dam. They were so far away it was difficult to detect any movement about them. But now that he looked closer, Longarm saw a thin tracery of smoke escaping from one chimney.

"How many are guarding the dam?"

"A complement of at least twenty. They patrol the dam and the surrounding country. The reason we haven't been spotted by now is the patrol is probably on the other side of the canyon."

"Where's the spillway?"

"It's below us. You can't see it from this ridge."

"How do you know all this, Tyler?"

"I spent two years up here guarding this dam from the Apaches."

"Apaches?"

"Sure. When the colonel first arrived here, there was a small settlement of Apaches in this wing of the canyon. Some Kiowas, too."

"But no longer?"

Tyler shrugged. "That's right."

"I think we'd better get back and call a meeting.

We've got some plans to make. Things to do." Longarm grinned at Tyler. "Hell, it looks like maybe I'm not going to stay trapped in this corner of hell for the rest of my life, after all."

As Longarm turned his mount, Tyler said, "What've you got in mind?"

"I'll tell you later," Longarm replied. "Right now, we got some hard riding to do."

Longarm lifted his mount to a gallop. With a shrug, Tyler kept pace, the rest trailing behind.

As he rode, Longarm found it difficult to believe that what he was thinking had not occurred to Tyler or any of the others—until it dawned on him that the hardest thing to see sometimes is the nose on your face.

Four days later, Longarm had managed to gather all the ranchers together in Lyman Billings's new place. They could not use his kitchen this time. It was too small. But they were able to gather around a long deal table Lyman brought out to the barn. Ed Munger, Simon Waller, Coop Hamner, and Wes Thompson were there, along with Tyler and his men—and Cecil Benton, who had only recently allowed he was well enough to be up and about. Benton kept to himself in a corner, arms folded, eyes averted.

As usual, the women had turned it into a family get-together and were busy loading more tables in the yard with enough vittles to make each of them groan aloud in despair. As the men exchanged greetings and got themselves settled in the cool barn, the shrill cries of the children playing outside in the yard came through the barn's thin walls.

Juanita and the woman Tyler was now sweet on,

154·

Wes's youngest daughter Amanda, brought in coffee and corn liquor. As soon as the men had tasted whichever they preferred, Longarm brought the meeting to order by getting to his feet and clearing his throat.

"I suppose," he began, "that most of you gents are bettin' the colonel is satisfied now—that he's going to be perfectly willing to leave you be up here amidst the prickly pear and the salt cedar, in the land of the rattlesnake and the scorpion."

"You know damn well he won't do nothin' of the sort, Long," drawled Simon Waller. "But we ain't about to curl up and die, neither. Let him come. This is mean country to fight a war in, and he knows that, too."

"It is," Longarm agreed.

"Out with it, Long," Ed Munger barked, his yellow mustache drooping more radically than before. His running skirmish with the colonel's troops had resulted in a severe wound. As a result he had lost the use of his left arm, but it did not appear to have slowed him down much. "You didn't bring us over here to tell us what we already know. Tyler tells me you got a plan to stop the son of a bitch."

"That's what Long had before," said Coop Hamner, his raw face growing dark with anger. "A plan to free the slaves and ruin the colonel. Now look at us!"

"Well, at least he got us some new recruits," drawled Wes Thompson, tipping his jug up, "even if they are darkies."

There was grim laughter at that, then an even grimmer silence as all eyes turned back to Longarm.

"Ed Munger is right," said Longarm. "I do have a plan. What surprises me is that none of you thought of it before I did."

155

"Out with it, Long," said Munger. "Maybe we just ain't as bright as you Yankee marshals."

Longarm shrugged. "Damned if it don't look that way. I'm talking about the colonel's reservoir, and the dam he built to hold all that water back. It's less than twenty miles from here, on the other side of the ridge. You men have always known of this reservoir. Am I right?"

"Sure we have," snapped Coop Hamner. "So what's that to you? Everyone remembers what it took to build that."

"Yes," Longarm agreed. "I suppose everyone does." He paused and looked about at each rancher, each sworn implacable enemy of the colonel—a man they had come to know as a ruthless, diabolical tyrant. "And yet, not one of you has ever thought of what it would mean to the colonel to lose that dam, to have those tons of water sent plunging on down that chute of a canyon all the way to the Rio Grande."

Longarm was right. They hadn't thought of such a thing. Not until that moment. They looked around at each other, stunned. In the corner, Cecil Benton uncrossed his arms and stood away from the wall.

"My God!" said Ed Munger, his voice hushed. "That would wipe out everything!"

"The town, the fields, all them people!" said Wes, astounded.

Simon Waller slapped his hand down onto the table. "But it sure as hell would finish the colonel!"

"Which means I'm for it," growled Munger.

"Hold it," said Coop Hamner. "Hold it right there. What Long's proposin' is a damn sight easier to think on than to do. That dam is guarded night and day."

156

That sobered them up somewhat and they looked back at Longarm.

"I know all about the contingent stationed at the dam," Longarm told them. "Lieutenant Tyler was once stationed there himself. From what he tells me, I don't reckon we're going to have all that much trouble dealin' with them soldiers. But that ain't the problem."

"Well, what is, then?" asked Munger, twirling his yellowing mustache, his eyes gleaming expectantly.

"We need something to blow the dam."

"Gunpowder would do it," broke in Tyler. "Or dynamite."

"Where the hell you goin' to get that?" demanded Coop Hamner.

"I propose to send someone to the army post in Sutpen to steal what dynamite the colonel has left in the arsenal building there," Longarm said. "Tyler knows the post like the back of his hand. I've got two former slaves who are willing to go back with someone, and I've chosen the man I think can handle the job."

"Who?" Coop demanded.

"Benton. Cecil Benton. It's the only way he can prove to me—and to the rest of us—that he's no longer a stooge of the colonel. It is also the only way he can assure himself a chance to escape this place, and get back to civilization where a man of his stripe can function properly."

"I resent that, damn you!" snarled Benton, approaching the table.

"You willing to lead this mission?" Munger drawled, his eyes narrowed in suspicion.

Benton moistened his lips. He felt the cold eyes on

him. These men all knew of his previous perfidy, his disastrous attempt to curry favor with the colonel by turning Longarm and Tyler in. He, along with Tyler, had suffered miserably for that folly, but it was still difficult for any of them to accept him. For weeks, Benton had been withering under Billings's unspoken contempt.

Longarm was counting on the young man's desire to gain their acceptance. He was hoping also that Benton was finally ready to grow up and show some backbone.

Benton looked around at each hostile face, then turned to Longarm. "All right," he said with some defiance, "I'll lead that party in. I'll get you your precious dynamite. And when I do, I'll expect some respect."

Longarm nodded briskly. "You bring back that dynamite, Benton, and you'll have all the respect you'll ever want."

"That's the truth, Benton," Munger promised.

There were a few more grudging agreements as Longarm held up his hand to silence them. "All right," he said. "It's settled then. We blow the colonel's dam."

The next night Longarm and the rest watched Benton pull out. He had Ned and another former slave with him. Ned and his companion rode in the wagon; Benton was astride a black, leading two pack horses.

The plan, as explained patiently to Benton by Tyler and Longarm that day, was for Benton to hide the wagon as close as possible to Sutpen, then move in at night with the two pack horses, using them to carry the dynamite back to the wagon. They were to travel only at night, and Benton was being given a week to complete the mission. By the time he pulled out, the young man was fairly confident of success and was indeed quite cocky. Everyone had been working at the task of convincing him what a simple, but vital, mission it was.

As soon as Benton was out of sight, Longarm moved back to the barn with the others to set their portion of the plan in operation.

For two days, Longarm and Tyler reconnoitered the approaches to the dam, while noting the routine of the soldiers guarding it. Early on, Tyler thought he had been spotted, but nothing came of it, and soon the two men had a pretty clear idea of how they were going to manage their assault. The best time for the attack on the twin garrisons, it was agreed, would be in the early hours of the morning, when most of the soldiers were asleep and only two sentries were assigned to guard the approaches to the dam.

Longarm and his men had the task of attacking the far side of the dam, then moving across its top to join with Tyler in his assault on the near side. Accordingly, his was the largest band, since the garrison at the far end was open and more vulnerable, and thus held far more troops than the one closer. Even more important, it was this garrison which contained the arsenal. And that meant gunpowder—barrels of it.

Now, an hour before midnight, they were poised to strike. There were fourteen men in all—nine with Longarm and three under Tyler's command. With a wave to Tyler, who was watching from a distance, Longarm led his men over the ridge. By the time they reached the canyon floor, the moon had sunk well below the canyon wall, leaving them in almost total darkness. With only the dim light of the stars to show them the way, they had to pick their way through acres of mesquite. When at last they reached the far side of the canyon, many of

Longarm's men had suffered severe scratches and scrapes from brushing or stumbling against the trees' treacherous thorns.

Longarm found the narrow trail he had discovered earlier during his reconnoitering of the dam and led his men up it until he was on a level with the garrison. It stood at the base of the dam less than twenty feet from them when they finished climbing up the trail. A steep path led from the rear of the garrison building up onto the dam.

As his men crowded around him, Longarm looked up at the stars to gain some idea of the time. From the position of the Dipper, he realized it was now well past midnight. Longarm sent three men up onto the dam to deal with the sentry patrolling there, waited a moment, then led his men toward the garrison building. There was supposed to be another sentry, his patrol area the base of the dam.

With Sam Bigger at his side, Longarm reached the outside wall of the garrison building, then worked his way around the corner to the door. As he did so, he saw the sentry a few hundred feet below the garrison, sitting with his back to the base of the dam, his rifle leaning against his shoulder.

"I will get that one," Sam whispered.

Longarm nodded. As Sam moved silently off down the slope, Longarm glanced up at the rim of the dam. He could see and hear nothing, but he had to assume that the three men would be able to take care of the remaining sentry.

Longarm moved closer to the door, turned the knob, then pushed it open. He was not surprised to find it unlocked. Since the Apaches and Kiowas had been wiped out, the colonel had no reason to believe the dam would ever be under attack again. As Tyler had explained to Longarm, the post was now not much more than a training base for the colonel's newest and rawest recruits.

There was a single table in the entrance hall with a lamp on it. The lamp's wick was turned well down, and the light it gave off was barely enough to show the dimensions of the table itself. Tyler had explained to Longarm where the sleeping quarters were. Longarm led his men through a door to his right.

The long line of bunks was barely visible in the dimness. Longarm waited until his men had drifted over to take their places in front of them before lifting the lantern he had taken from the table and turning up the wick. As the glow increased, they were able to see the bunks clearly.

They were all empty.

Chapter 11

Longarm snuffed out the lantern and yelled to his men, "Get out!" It was a trap.

But his warning came too late as the garrison's troops burst into the building behind them. Longarm rushed back through the door to the other room, his .44 blazing. He was met by a ragged, startled fusillade from the soldiers and dove behind the table, overturning it to give himself cover.

Only a few of the soldiers had reentered the building to spring their trap when Longarm burst back into the entrance hall—and two of them had been immediately cut down by Longarm's fire. Three or four fled back out the door, leaving at the most three soldiers hovering fearfully in the darkness to battle it out with Longarm and his men. Counting on their inexperience under fire, Longarm continued to pour fire at them while he called out to his men to make a break for it.

But only two men followed Longarm out of the sleeping quarters, and one of them was cut down as he attempted to reach the overturned table. The one who managed to reach Longarm was Coop Hamner, and he was swearing a blue streak as he kept up a rapid fire into the corners and other dark places of the room.

The outside door opened and three more of the garrison troops poured in. Nudging Coop to give him a hand, Longarm grabbed the wounded man under his arm and dragged him back into the sleeping quarters, firing as he went.

There was no hope for it, Longarm realized. He and Tyler must have been spotted earlier while they were reconnoitering the dam. The outpost's commandant had been smart enough to give no indication they had been seen, but had simply lain low and waited for the attack.

Longarm heard rifle fire from outside and the sound of men crying out in panic. It must be Tyler, he realized. Something had alerted him to the trap, and he was attacking to relieve the pressure on Longarm's men.

"Let's go!" Longarm cried. "That's Tyler out there. Get ready to move out."

Crouching by the doorway to the sleeping quarters, Longarm saw the outer door burst open, just as he finished reloading his Colt.

"Now!" he cried, leading his men back into the outer room.

Halfway to the door, as the men raced across the room with him, Longarm saw the huge figure of Sam Bigger standing in the doorway, his Winchester in his hand, pumping merciless fire into the few soldiers still huddled in the room's shadows.

Longarm was astounded. Sam Bigger, all by himself, was the source of their relief. Even as Longarm reached Bigger, the black man dropped his rifle and slumped back against the doorjamb. But his job was done. The soldiers inside were out of action—and the way out of the trap was clear.

As Longarm burst out of the garrison, he saw more soldiers rushing up the slope toward them. Flinging up his Colt, he went down on one knee and began firing carefully and low. The onrushing troops dove for cover.

"Onto the dam!" Longarm cried as he got to his feet and flung himself around the building and headed for the steep path.

Once Longarm reached the path that ran along the top of the dam, he came upon the bodies of the three men he had sent to take care of the sentry. One had a fatal saber wound in his gut and the other two had been clubbed down viciously from behind. Longarm could only wonder how Sam Bigger had been able to elude the trap that sentry sitting back against the dam must have set for him.

There was sporadic gunfire from the other side of the dam by this time. Tyler and his small band had their hands full as well, it seemed. Their best bet was to fight their way across the top of the dam, join up with Tyler, and hope to hell they could make it over the ridge to safety.

The only difficulty in that course, Longarm realized, were the wounded. Could they keep up? Under no circumstances would Longarm contemplate letting the colonel or his men take captives. As his men directed a nuisance fire down on the regrouping forces below them in the darkness, Longarm checked on the condition of his wounded.

Four men were hurt, one seriously. That was Sam Bigger. He had an enormous hole in his chest and was breathing with some difficulty. Sudden, tearing spells of coughing racked him, and each time blood came up. The other wounded man had a thigh wound, around which he had tied a bandanna. He assured Longarm that he was able to move. The remaining wounded suffered from flesh wounds, one to the forearm and the other to his side. Both wounds were painful but manageable.

Ed Munger was hovering over Sam Bigger. He glanced up as Longarm returned to the black man's side.

"He ain't goin' to make it, Long," Munger rasped. "He's got a hole in him bigger than my fist. I don't know how in hell he was able to make it up that incline to the garrison."

"I don't either, but he did."

Bigger opened his eyes. "Got you out, did I?"

"That you did," Longarm replied.

The man chuckled, despite his coughing. ". . . heard the scramble up here when they went after them three you sent . . . gave me warnin' . . ." He shook his head slightly. ". . . should'a ducked faster . . ."

"Now, you're gonna be all right, Sam," said Munger. "You just stay still and we'll take care of you."

Sam Bigger looked up at him and slowly shook his head. "I'm gonna see . . . my woman . . . ain't gonna stay this place . . . no more . . ."

His powerful head lolled forward.

"Damn!" muttered Munger. "Oh, damn!"

Longarm thought fleetingly of Hattie, Samantha's

cook. She had hoped this big black would think of her, maybe even take her home with him and wrap his big arms about her. Well, there was no chance of that now.

Longarm left Munger with Sam Bigger and crabbed over to the edge of the dam to look down. The darkness below them was alive with the flash of gunfire. He told his men to cease fire to save their ammunition, then gathered them around him. They were going to have to make it across the dam, Longarm told them, while two men stayed behind to serve as a rear guard.

Coop Hamner volunteered. So did his son, Jeff. Longarm was reluctant to see a father and son take such a chance, but he did not feel he was in any position to argue. One thing he was sure of: Coop and his son would make an excellent rear guard. He had watched the two of them knocking cans off a fence one day.

They moved out. Halfway across the dam, Longarm saw figures, bent low, racing toward them. For just an instant he thought it might be more of the troops guarding the dam, but he soon caught sight of Tyler in the lead and hunkered down to wait for them to reach him.

"Jesus!" Tyler cried when he reached Longarm. "It was a trap. Them sons of bitches were waiting for us."

"They caught sight of us earlier, I figure."

"Well, we were luckier than you, looks like. I caught sight of them moving about in the brush outside the guardhouse setting up the trap, so I sent my men into the brush after them." He chuckled. "The surprise was on them."

"You're right, we weren't so lucky. Sam Bigger is dead and we got three wounded."

"So what now?"

"We were coming over to join you and give you a

hand. But here you are, so you can give us a hand. We'll play it your way. Keep some men up here to continue firing on those still below us—I figure there must be at least five or six left—while we go down there after them individually, the way you did."

Tyler nodded and turned to one of his men, who in turn chose three others. The four men, keeping low, raced back to the other end of the dam to join Coop and his son.

A moment later, as the reinforced band began peppering the darkness below them, Longarm and Tyler led their men back across the top of the dam, then down once more into the black canyon. Crossing the spillway drenched them, but it was the long, painful trek through the same mesquite that had done such a job on Longarm's men earlier that caused the most grumbling. But they kept it down and soon they were moving as silently as shadows up the slope behind the colonel's men. Longarm caught a gunflash off to his right, tapped Tyler on the shoulder, and slipped off toward it.

The fellow he was stalking got off two more shots before Longarm reached him. A twig snapped under Longarm's elbow, alerting his quarry. As the soldier turned, Longarm hurled himself through the brush and bore the fellow down beneath him, his right hand clapped firmly over his mouth. The man began to struggle powerfully. Unable to release him for fear that he would cry out, Longarm stood up, dragging the man to his feet after him. With both hands now clapped firmly over the soldier's mouth, Longarm kept lifting until the fellow's feet were off the ground. Then he shook him like a terrier might shake a rat until he heard the man's neck snap.

As the soldier collapsed silently to the ground, Longarm ducked back into the brush and kept moving.

The firing by Longarm's men from atop the dam was desultory but dangerous as occasional rounds pounded into the slope just ahead or just behind him. He caught another gunflash, this one to his left and further up the slope. Keeping low, he snaked up the incline as far as he could go and waited. A curse exploded just to his left, followed by the sound of a revolver being cocked. The detonation that followed almost deafened Longarm as the fellow he had been tracking fired up at one of Longarm's men who was momentarily silhouetted against the night sky.

Longarm moved carefully to the left and, almost before he knew it, he found himself staring into the pale, astonished face of a sergeant. The man's yellow chevrons seemed to leap out of the darkness at Longarm.

Instinctively, the sergeant lashed down with the barrel of his revolver, catching Longarm on the side of the face, stunning him. The sergeant jumped up then and kicked furiously at Longarm, catching him in the side and sending him tumbling down the slope. As Longarm felt himself turning and tumbling ass over teakettle down the slope, he tried desperately to slow his punishing progress down the hill and managed finally to grab hold of a shrub. He hung on to it grimly and his body stopped tumbling. But his head still rocked and the slope and sky exchanged places with sickening frequency as he shook his head in an effort to steady his senses.

The sergeant, on his feet by this time, was charging down the slope after Longarm, anxious to finish him off. In his right hand he still held his revolver; that much

Longarm could see, no matter how violently the universe spun about him. He closed his eyes and stuck his right hand down into his boot. Nothing. He moved his hand around more, caught the small butt, and pulled the derringer free. As he raised it, Longarm opened his eyes and saw the sergeant sliding to a halt in front of him. The world was still spinning, but not so badly. When the barrel and the sergeant's chest coincided, Longarm squeezed off a shot.

The slug stamped a neat hole in the sergeant's tunic. The man sat down quickly. But his own revolver was still in his hand, and still pointing at Longarm. Longarm rolled aside a second before the sergeant squeezed the trigger. The round missed and when Longarm glanced back he saw that the sergeant was now leaning peacefully back against the slope, the revolver on the ground beside him.

The exchange of fire brought the sound of running feet. Longarm crawled swiftly away into the brush and kept low as first one, then two cavalrymen raced past. A moment later, both of them were blasted out of their boots, and Tyler, holding a smoking gun, stood up in plain view on the slope just above him.

"That's the last of them, I reckon," Tyler called over to Longarm. "You can come out now, Marshal!"

Brushing himself off and shaking his aching head, Longarm got to his feet and walked somewhat sheepishly over to join Tyler. Tyler yelled up to his men on the dam to cease fire, then called out to those he and Longarm had brought with them. It took a while for them all to gather round. They looked somewhat the worse for wear, and two did not return at all, no matter how many times Longarm and others called.

One of the missing was Simon Waller's oldest boy. The other was Ed Munger.

The first rays of the sun were breaking over the canyon's rim when Tyler succeeded in breaking through the armory door. He stepped aside to let Longarm see what was inside. The lawman was not disappointed. At least twenty barrels of gunpowder were stacked along one wall. After a diligent search, Longarm found the lengths of fuse he would need. He examined the fuse carefully. It was Bickford fuse, famous for burning almost exactly one foot in thirty seconds, but this was an old fuse—and the last thing Longarm wanted was a hangfire. He felt a little more confident when his inspection revealed no breaks at all in the gutta-percha wrapping used to lock out moisture. Pronouncing himself satisfied, he set the men to work removing the barrels of gunpowder, while he left the armory to inspect the dam.

The front of the dam was constructed like a Kentucky fort. The cottonwood logs that held the earthen dam in place were set in the ground like huge stakes, the entire structure braced a second time with a series of cottonwood logs, set into the ground at an angle. These buttressing logs were of greater than usual girth, and at their base stakes had been driven into the ground to anchor them securely.

The first order of business, Longarm had already concluded during his reconnaissance of the dam, was to knock the buttresses free. To that end the men had brought plenty of axes with them. Even while the gunpowder was being lugged from the arsenal, the sound of ringing axes echoed in the canyon. By midday all of the buttresses had been chopped through and knocked aside.

Longarm, standing on the rim of the dam when the last buttress was sent crashing, felt not a tremor pass through the solid earthen dam beneath his feet. In that instant he almost despaired of accomplishing his purpose. But he shook aside his misgivings and continued to direct the digging for what would soon be the fifth blast hole.

He was concentrating his charges in the center of the dam. This was obviously its weakest point since here, at its greatest height, it had the greatest volume of water to hold back. He was directing the men to dig the holes at least six feet deep because the lake's water level was quite high at this time, and this would enable him to set off the charges at least a foot below the water line.

By the end of the noon hour Longarm had set his charges atop the dam and was working feverishly on those he was placing at its base, again at the center of the structure. In order to insure that his charges generated enough power, he had directed the men to chop through the cottonwood logs to create blast holes that extended deep into the dam.

By mid-afternoon all of Longarm's charges had been set. In each case, he had fashioned a protective cylinder of bark, through which he threaded the fuse, enabling him to use fresh mud to pack around the barrels and stem the holes.

Now all they had to do was wait.

It was Coop's son, Jeff, who finally asked the inevitable question. "Mr. Long, why are we waitin' here like this? Ain't you got all your charges set?"

Longarm looked past Jeff at his father. "You want to tell him, Coop?"

"We're waitin' for the colonel, son," Coop drawled.

"Leastways, that's what the marshal here says. It's what you call a gamble—but a mighty long shot, if you ask me."

Jeff looked back at Long, and a few of the others who had not been made privy to Longarm's scheme drew closer, anxious for an explanation. After what they had been through, Longarm was not reluctant to provide one. "We sent Benton to get the gunpowder. But we didn't need him to do that," he pointed out. "Wouldn't you say that was true?"

Those gathered around Longarm agreed.

"Well, why did you send him, then?" Jeff asked.

Longarm smiled. "We sent Benton so he could betray us."

Jeff and the others looked at Longarm in astonishment. They had difficulty believing their ears. "You must be joshing, Mr. Long," Jeff said.

"Nope. 'Fraid not. What we are hoping is that Benton will tell the colonel we plan to attack the dam. We told Benton in a week. So that would give the colonel plenty of time—with Benton's help—to come marching up here to save the dam."

"But suppose the colonel don't come himself?" one of the others asked. "Suppose he just sends his men?"

"That's exactly the question I been askin' myself," said Coop.

Lieutenant Tyler had strolled over to join them by this time. The rest of the men were gathering around as well. "I know the colonel," Tyler told young Jeff. "This here dam is his pride and joy. He'll be up here himself with most of his men. He won't leave it to someone else to save the single most important structure in this canyon of his."

"Which way do you think he'll be coming?"

"The most direct trail from Sutpen to this dam is through the canyon, following that road down there alongside the canal. That's the way he'll be coming, I'm thinking."

"And we figured," said Munger, finishing up, "that he'd be in sight by now. That's why we been whalin' our tails off today."

"But what about the men you sent with Benton?" persisted Jeff. "Suppose they stop him from going to the colonel?"

"They were told to watch him closely and make a break as soon as he made any move to betray us. They were expecting him to do just that. One of them is going to warn the blacks in shanty town what's coming, and the other is going to warn a very good friend of mine in Sutpen."

"She wouldn't happen to have red hair, would she?" asked Tyler with a grin.

"She might," responded Longarm.

It was close to four o'clock when it became apparent that Cecil Benton had once again betrayed Longarm.

A cheer went up as soon as the lookout posted on the ridge alerted Longarm. Colonel Sutpen's column had just been spotted in the canyon below. So as not to warn the colonel that the dam had already been taken, the lookout—on Tyler's suggestion—had used a mirror to flash this intelligence to Longarm, Apache-style.

That left it all up to Longarm and Tyler. The lieutenant was assigned the task of lighting the fuses at the base of the dam, while Longarm took care of those charges atop it. Longarm was hoping they could manage to set off all the charges as close as possible to each other. But, if his rough calculations had any validity, it would be the charges on top of the dam that would provide the final tip of the scale.

On the other hand, the dam might hold.

But Longarm was not thinking of that as the men fled toward the ridge and Longarm peered down the canyon at the approaching troops. Yes; there he was, riding at the head of the column—Colonel Bascom Sutpen. The colonel was aboard his white charger, resplendent in his black felt Jeff Davis campaign hat, his buff silk net sash wound about his waist, the late-afternoon sun glinting off his steel scabbard.

Closer he rode, his cavalry right behind, his foot soldiers strung out somewhat wearily to the rear. Longarm had decided he would not give the signal to light the fuses until the colonel and his men were close enough for him to see the colonel's face. But, as he watched the approaching column, he felt a pang when he thought of all those young soldiers and the awesome destruction that would follow when he blew the dam. He consoled himself with the thought that many of those below him in the canyon would escape.

But not, he hoped, the author of this madness—Colonel Sutpen.

Chapter 12

With a burst of irritation Longarm twisted his head away, then realized the sentry he had posted on the ridge was using his mirror to gain Longarm's attention.

Shading his eyes, Longarm glanced up at the ridge and swore softly.

The colonel was no fool. He had sent a scouting party in advance of his main force, and at that moment it was moving along the ridge above the canyon. In a matter of minutes its members would be in a position to open fire on Longarm. That they hadn't already done so only meant that they hadn't yet spotted him. When they did open fire, the colonel would know the dam was already in rebel hands, and all bets would be off.

"Tyler!" Longarm called down to the lieutenant.

"Now! Light the fuses now!"

"Right!"

Longarm had cut the fuses long enough to give them plenty of time to flee the area, but he could not help reminding himself that these fuses were old. Some holes were going to blow sooner than others. Using his pocket knife, Longarm began splitting the ends of the fuses. Once he had prepared them all, he lit a short length of Bickford fuse to use as an igniter. At once it began spurting out a tiny, steady jet of flame. Igniting the fuses, Longarm waited a moment to make sure each one was lit, then dropped the igniter and started running for the ridge. He could hear Tyler pounding along behind him, anxious to overtake him, it seemed.

They were almost clear of the dam when the colonel's patrol spotted them and opened fire. The ground at his feet began exploding and the high whine of ricocheting bullets filled the air. Longarm kept running, but as he did so, he glanced down the canyon. As he had feared, the sudden eruption of gunfire from the ridge alerted the colonel and his troops, and Longarm could see them breaking for cover.

At that moment, Longarm's men waiting on the ridge opened fire on the colonel's patrol. The soldiers pulled back to concentrate on defending themselves, and a moment later, Longarm and Tyler had leaped from the dam to the slope and were clawing their way up its steep side, heading for the ridge.

They were halfway there when the gunpowder detonated. The ground under Longarm shifted slightly as the force of the blast slapped him forward into the slope. At that moment, all Longarm could hear was a high, ringing sound—and he was having difficulty drawing his breath.

Nevertheless, he managed to turn about and look down. He had expected to see the dam disintegrating under the surging push of the water as it spewed through the breach the blasts had opened.

But there was no breach.

Great chunks of the earthen dam were missing, and the water behind it—now a dark, muddy color—was churning angrily. But the dam still held. The only damage Longarm could see was to the spillway. Its gate seemed to have been jammed open, and a greater than usual volume of water was pouring through.

But that was the extent of the damage.

Longarm glanced down the canyon. The colonel had seen that his dam had held. Jubilant, he was leading his cavalry in a charge up the canyon toward the dam, his foot soldiers trailing far behind by this time as most of them remained on the slopes, content to let their colonel display whatever heroics the situation required.

Tyler scrambled closer. "I saw it, Longarm!" he cried. "All your barrels didn't go off! How many did you plant up there?"

"Five." Longarm had difficulty hearing, and his voice sounded strangely distant.

"Hell, Long, only three went off. So help me!"

Longarm looked back at the dam. The center of it had sagged considerably, and there were sections that appeared to have been blasted free of the dam itself, but in the central portion, especially, near the edge closest to the water, there had obviously been no detonation.

Once more Longarm glanced down the canyon. The colonel was almost close enough for Longarm to see his face. Unholstering his .44, Longarm pushed himself back down the slope, slipping and sliding recklessly until he was able to leap across to the dam. He was only dimly aware of gunfire and the whine of ricocheting bullets as he ran along the dam.

When he reached the two blast holes, he went down on one knee and pulled out the two fuses. Both of them had hung fire. He flung them away angrily and thought a moment. He had no fuses with him. All he had was his gun. Again he glanced down the canyon at the hard-charging colonel. It was a shame, Longarm thought. That son of a bitch came all this way for nothing.

In that instant, Longarm made up his mind. With both hands he dug out most of the packing above the barrels. Then he stood up and trotted past the two blow holes, turned and ran back the way he had come. As he raced over the undetonated barrels, he fired down at them in rapid succession.

The blast lifted him high into the air. He felt himself turning lazily. The sky exchanged places with the earth. He felt his right shoulder crunch down on something hard and unyielding. Then he was under water, twisting and turning, gasping for air. He was dimly aware of a thunderous, rushing sound as the water tugged at him strongly, threatening to pull him still further into its churning depths. He thought his lungs would burst. He reached out blindly. His hand caught hold of solid ground and he pulled himself out of the water. But the ground under his feet was unsteady, treacherous. In a night-marish way, it appeared to be falling away from under him.

Glancing back, he saw a great hole yawning open less than a foot behind him, a swirling torrent of water digging at it. He turned and ran. Twice he fell, but he was on his feet even before he stopped rolling. It was like a dream he used to have as a child—in which the faster he ran, the less ground he covered. Glancing ahead of him, he had the uncanny feeling that the slope of the ridge was receding before him, and that no matter how fast he ran, he could never reach it.

With one last, desperate lunge, he leaped for the sanctuary of the cliffside. Landing hard, he scrabbled frantically for something to grab hold of, and found a pine root. Panting violently, he looked back to see the dam breaking into huge chunks as it was caught up in the bursting torrent. Glancing down the canyon, he saw the first dark tide of the flood waters mounting the flue-like shunt, then rushing down the other side. If anything, the onrushing tongue of water seemed to have gained speed and destructive force as it swept on into the main canyon.

Longarm watched numbly for a moment as Tyler and someone else slid down the slope to his side and began to pull him back up to the ridge.

His head felt as if it had swollen to twice its normal size, but he shook off the sensation and looked up at Tyler. "The colonel! Did we get him?"

"You did it, Marshal! You got the son of a bitch! He's gone, with most of his cavalry. The rest of his troops saw it coming and got away."

Longarm closed his eyes and fell back. A numbness was moving up through his thighs, gradually claiming his entire body. Before he reached the ridge, he drifted off into blackness.

Juanita was leaning close over him, placing cold compresses on his forehead. A cold light was filtering into the room. Juanita's father was at the foot of the bed, watching mournfully. As Longarm glanced his way, the

181

old man crossed himself devoutly and his lips began to move in prayer. Beside him stood Pepe, looking as sorrowful and pensive as his father. Juanita kissed his cheek, then stepped away. He thought he saw tears moving down her face.

Then he moved his head slightly to look out through the dim window and drifted off once again...

A blanket over his knees, Longarm sat on the veranda of Juan Lopez de Santa Rosa's hacienda, and listened for the second time that day as Juanita recounted to him the events that had closed out Colonel Bascom Sutpen's empire.

Once the colonel and most of his cavalry had been swept to their deaths, his soldiers offered no further resistance. When, less than a week later, the settlers and ranchers moved down out of the hills, they found that Sutpen, the irrigated fields, and almost all sign of what the colonel had built had been swept away. The flood's devastation had been complete.

Because of the warning Longarm had sent with Ned and the other man, however, most of the blacks had slipped away onto higher ground, and Samantha and a few of her friends had been able to move swiftly enough to find refuge on the roadway Sutpen had carved out of the mountainside.

It was along this steep road that the long flood of ex-slaves and survivors toiled as they fled the devastated valley in the days that followed. Once they crossed the Rio Grande over the colonel's drawbridge, they poured into Mexico. Some went westward and recrossed the Rio to regroup in Presidio. Others stayed in Mexico, fleshing out the towns of Matamoros, San Vicente, and San Carlos.

Since the survivors, ex-slaves and whites, had a strange story to tell indeed, they found themselves made welcome everywhere.

"And you are welcome to stay here, Longarm," Juanita said hopefully. "You must not talk of going back to Denver. Here you can stay. My father, he say you are very brave man. He be proud to have you as his son. Pepe, too, he want you to stay."

"And you, Juanita?"

She smiled and leaned forward to kiss him on the mouth. "You know how I feel, señor."

After the way she had awakened him that morning, he knew how she felt, and how he felt as well.

It was a sweet prospect, indeed, staying with these warm, hospitable people. Before he was able to use his limbs once again, he had considered what it would be like to remain in this land with Juanita and had almost convinced himself that he could be content. But now he was fine again, and soon he would be walking and riding as well as before. He knew this for a certainty. He had felt the power surging back into his limbs these past few days—this morning, especially.

"I must go back, Juanita. I am a lawman. That is what I do. And, thanks to the care you have lavished on me these past weeks, I will be able to return to that task. I am sorry. You understand, don't you?"

Tears gleamed in her eyes. "I understand," she said. "You are a man and must do what you must do. And I am just a woman. I must let you do what you want."

He reached for her. She moved close into his arms,

and as he hugged her to him, he wondered if maybe he wasn't crazy to insist on returning to Denver.

Three weeks later, as he stepped out of Denver's famous Windsor Hotel, Longarm asked himself that same question again. Bearing down on him in the company of a beautiful auburn-haired girl he knew only as Jeanette and a well-dressed, very distinguished gentleman who could only be his father was Cecil Benton.

Longarm had difficulty believing the evidence of his senses. As Benton hurried toward him, he didn't know if he should reach for his Colt or run.

"My dear Longarm!" Benton cried. "What a delightful surprise!"

Grabbing Longarm's hand, Benton shook it with great warmth and enthusiasm as he introduced Longarm to his recent bride and to his father, Senator Benton.

"You must join us in a drink to celebrate," young Benton insisted.

Longarm saw no polite way to refuse, and followed them back into the hotel. They found a quiet table in the saloon and sat down as Benton, eager to recount his exploits once again, went over for Longarm's benefit the various heroic deeds he had performed in saving so many from the devastating flood Longarm had loosed upon Colonel Sutpen and his doomed community.

"Then you did not go straight to the colonel and tell him what I had planned?" Longarm asked coldly as he sipped his whiskey.

"Upon my word of honor, sir, I did not."

"What happened, then? How did the colonel know what we were about? Why did he march up that canyon to stop us?"

"Those two you sent with me disappeared as soon as they got close to the army post. That left it to me alone to break into the arsenal. I am afraid I botched things miserably and was stopped by soldiers as I was loading the pack horses."

"I see. The colonel tortured you and made you tell."

"No. Fortunately, it was not that way at all. I convinced the soldiers to release me if I told them something that would assure their survival. Then I told them that you planned to destroy the dam, that your men were already in position and that, one way or another, you would get the job done."

"They released you when you told them that?"

Benton leaned closer. "They were men of honor, Longarm. Besides, you have no idea how pleased they were to learn that there was a force ready to send this colonel to hell and gone. Yes, they let me go."

"And then they told the colonel what we planned?"

Benton shrugged. "They must have had a change of heart." He leaned back and smiled. "Of course I knew you would blow the dam in any case. There was no question of that."

Longarm leaned back and regarded Benton coolly, thoughtfully. This man had tried to kill him on more than one occasion. Indeed, the only thing anyone who knew him could be certain of was his perfidy. By rights, Longarm should now find himself anxious to bring Benton to account for his many outrages. Yet here he was, calmly letting Benton relate the most outrageous version Longarm could have imagined of what had happened when he was sent after that gunpowder. On the other hand, Longarm had to admit that Benton's account was so incredible it just might be true.

Yet what did any of it matter now? Captain Miles Winthrop's strange tale had been verified; the illegal border trade originating in Matamoros had been halted without the Federal government having to send troops onto Mexican territory. And Colonel Bascom Sutpen was dead.

Longarm finished his drink and stood up.

"Must you go so soon, Marshal?" asked Senator Benton pleasantly.

"I was on my way to the gaming tables when your son accosted me," Longarm lied. "Now I must be off. It was a pleasure meeting you, Senator." He glanced at the girl. "And you again, Jeanette. My congratulations to you both."

Longarm touched the brim of his hat to them and left. Once outside, he lit a cheroot and inhaled deeply. Going over Benton's account once more in his mind, he began to chuckle as he realized that the most amazing feature of this adventure was not the mad colonel and his tight little Confederacy, but the incredible durability of one Cecil Benton.

Still chuckling, Longarm strode off in search of a poker game—or perhaps something even more pleasant.

Watch for

LONGARM AND THE SNAKE DANCERS

fifty-first novel in the bold LONGARM series
from Jove

coming in January!